The Wild Ride
and Other Scottish Stories

The Wild Ride
and Other Scottish Stories

CHOSEN BY GORDON JARVIE

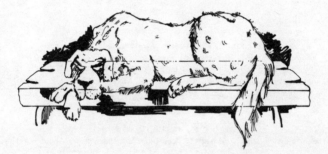

ILLUSTRATED BY
ELAINE MCGREGOR TURNEY

VIKING KESTREL

For Sally Jane and Andrew John in particular

VIKING KESTREL
Penguin Books Ltd, Harmondsworth, Middlesex, England
Viking Penguin Inc., 40 West 23rd Street, New York, New York 10010, U.S.A.
Penguin Books Australia Ltd, Ringwood, Victoria, Australia
Penguin Books Canada Limited, 2801 John Street, Markham, Ontario, Canada L3R 1B4
Penguin Books (N.Z.) Ltd, 182–190 Wairau Road, Auckland 10, New Zealand

First published 1986

This selection copyright © Gordon Jarvie, 1986
The Acknowledgements on page 145 constitute an extension of this copyright page
Illustrations copyright © Elaine McGregor Turney, 1986

British Library Cataloguing in Publication Data

The Wild Ride: and other Scottish Stories.
 – (Viking Kestrel fiction)
 1. Children's stories, English
 I. Jarvie, Gordon
 823'.01'089282 [J]   PZ5

ISBN 0–670–80987–X

Made and printed in Great Britain by
Richard Clay (The Chaucer Press) Ltd,
Bungay, Suffolk

Contents

Introduction

When I was at school in Edinburgh, it seemed difficult to find Scottish stories for young people that were not based on Scottish history or folklore or music-hall or a combination of these. After a while, I got too old for Tam Lin and Whuppity Stoorie, Angus Og and Rashin Coatie; to say nothing of Bonnie Dundee and Mary Queen of Scots, Oor Wullie and Wee MacGreegor. I wanted something more up to date in my reading, and more realism.

This collection mainly keeps off folklore and history, and offers a variety of modern stories. Not all of them were written especially for young readers, but they have all been enjoyed by readers of ten upwards. If you like funny stories, look out for 'The Consolation Prize', 'Jehovah's Joke', 'Grumphie', 'Icarus', or 'Touch and Go!'. If you like ghost stories, try the title story of this book, 'The Wild Ride in the Tilt Cart', or 'Sandy MacNeil and His Dog' — or if you're interested in 'second sight' or the paranormal, you'll perhaps enjoy 'Do You Believe in Ghosts?'. If, like me, you like stories about ordinary people set in the modern real-life world, try 'Silver Linings' — published here for the first time — and 'The Mystery of the Beehive' and 'Alicky's Watch'. A story from my parents' generation — and your grandparents' — is 'Three Fingers Are Plenty'. To appreciate it fully, you will have to try and imagine what it was like to grow up in a seaside village of fifty years ago, just before the Second World War.

All these stories are of course written by grown men and women, and a lot of them refer to *their* childhood. So several stories take us into a slightly bygone period, with references to the smithy and the croft, Jo Grimond and the *Queen Mary*, Alexander's big blue buses, and the tramlines at Newington.

It is interesting to compare some of the stories — 'Sunday Class' with 'The Blot', for instance, or 'Touch and Go!' with 'The Wild Geese'. The subjects are similar, but the treatment is not necessarily so.

These stories are all Scottish, but they should appeal to readers in other parts of the world as well as to young Scots. I hope you will find here authors whose writing you enjoy, and that having sampled it here, you will go on to look for more of it elsewhere. One good story should always lead to another.

G.J.
1986

The Wild Ride in the Tilt Cart

SORCHE NIC LEODHAS

There was a lad named Tommy Hayes and a more likeable lad
you'd never hope to see, for all that he was a Sassenach born
and bred. Tommy was the sort to take his fishing very seriously,
so when a Scottish friend wrote to him and invited him to
come up to his place in the Highlands for a visit and be sure to
bring his fishing gear, Tommy was delighted. He'd always
heard the fishing up where his friend lived was extra fine but
he'd never had a chance to try it before. So immediately he sent
a telegram to his friend to say he was coming and what time
they could expect him to get there. Then he packed up his
fishing gear and a few clothes in his bag, and off he went.

He stepped off the train just about nightfall into the midst of
teeming rain with the water coming down in bucketsful and
sloshing all over the place. The very first thing he discovered
was that nobody had come to meet him. The station was on
the edge of a small village, and there wasn't a soul in sight
except for the stationmaster, and he was inside the station
keeping out of the rain.

Tommy couldn't understand it for he'd sent the telegram in
plenty of time. He went in and asked the stationmaster if he
had seen anyone in the village from his friend's place, thinking
maybe they'd had an errand to do and would be coming along

9

The Wild Ride and Other Scottish Stories

for him later. But the stationmaster said that nobody at all had come over from that way for as good as a week. Tommy was surprised and maybe a little bit annoyed but he settled down in a corner of the station to wait for somebody to come and fetch him. He waited and waited and waited but nobody came at all, and after a while he found out why. The stationmaster came out of his bit of an office with a telegram in his hand. 'This is for the folk up where you're going,' he told Tommy. 'Maybe you'd not mind taking it along, since you're going there yourself.'

Tommy didn't have to read the telegram to know that it was the one he had sent to his friend. Well, that explained why nobody had come to meet his train. And what was more, nobody was going to come. Since the telegram hadn't been delivered, they wouldn't know at all that he was there.

'Och, well, 'tis a pity,' said the stationmaster. ''Twas early this morn I got it, and I'd have sent it along had anyone been passing by that was going in that direction. But what with the weather and all, there's few been out this day, and what there was, was bound the other way.'

Well, being a good-natured lad, Tommy couldn't see any sense in making a fuss about it. He'd just have to find a way for himself to get where he wanted to go.

The stationmaster was sorry for Tommy, but he could give him no help. There was nobody in the village who'd be able to take Tommy to his friend's house that night. Two or three folk had farm carts, but the beasts were all put up for the night and people were all in their beds. They wouldn't be likely to take it kindly if Tommy woke them out of their sleep.

'You could stay in the station o'ernight,' the man said. 'You'd be welcome to do so, if you liked to. Happen there'll be someone along on the morrow going the way you want to go.'

'And maybe not,' said Tommy, not feeling very hopeful. 'No, if I'm going to get there at all, I can see I'll have to walk.'

'Aye,' the stationmaster agreed. ''Tis a matter of five miles.'

'That's not too bad,' said Tommy, determined to be cheerful.

'Mostly up and down hill,' said the stationmaster glumly. 'The road is rough, forbye. And 'tis raining.'

10

'It can't be helped,' said Tommy. 'I'll just have to make the best of it.' He picked up his bag and started out into the rain. The stationmaster came to the door and pointed out the road Tommy was to take. Tommy had gone a little way when the man called out after him. 'Have a care for auld Rabbie MacLaren! I doubt he'll be out on the road the night.'

That didn't mean a thing to Tommy, so he just plodded along through the rain.

The stationmaster had told him no lies about the road. Tommy couldn't remember having trod a worse one. It was up and down hill all right. Tommy toiled along, splashing through the puddles and slipping on loose pebbles, with the rain pouring from the back of his hat brim down inside the collar of his coat. He was beginning to wonder if the fishing was going to be fine enough to pay for all the trouble he was going through to get it when he heard the sound of cart wheels rolling up the hill behind him.

He stopped and turned to look, and although it was growing dark he could make out the shape of a tilt cart coming towards him. It had a canvas top stretched over some sort of framework, and Tommy thought to himself that if he could get a lift he'd be out of the rain at any rate. He set his bag down and stood in the middle of the road, waving his arms and shouting.

'Will you give me a lift up the road?' called Tommy.

The driver did not answer but the cart came on swiftly, bumping along over the ruts in a heedless way. As it came up to him, Tommy called out again, 'Will you give me a lift?'

The man in the cart didn't say 'Aye', but he didn't say 'Nay'. The cart kept on rolling along and Tommy had to pick up his bag and jump to the side of the road to keep from being run down.

'I'll pay you well,' cried Tommy as he jumped. He felt rather desperate. The tilt cart was his only hope, for he doubted if he'd have another chance to get a lift that night. 'I'll pay you well!' said Tommy again.

The driver did not answer, but it seemed to Tommy that the horse that was drawing the cart slowed down a little. Tommy took that as a sign that his offer had been accepted. He picked up his bag and ran after the cart and hopped in beside the driver without waiting for the cart to come to a full stop.

As soon as Tommy was in the cart the horse picked up speed again. The creature didn't seem to be minding the roughness of the road in the least. It brought the cart up to the crest of the hill at a good round pace and, when they started down the other side, the horse stretched its legs and fairly flew. The cart bounced and bumped and jolted over the ruts and Tommy's teeth chattered with the shaking he was getting. All he could do was hold fast to the side of the cart and hope for the best. The cart wheels threw out sparks as they hit the stones that strewed the road, and every now and then a big one sent the cart a foot or more in the air. Uphill and downhill went Tommy with the cart, hanging on for dear life and expecting to land any minute in a heap in the ditch with horse, cart, and driver piled on top of him.

He plucked up enough courage after a while to attempt to implore the driver to slow down. He turned to look at the man beside him. What he saw took the words out of his mouth. It wasn't so much the sight of him, although that was bad enough. He was the hairiest creature Tommy had seen in his life. A wild thatch of hair grew over his head and down over his ears, and was met by a long grizzled beard that almost covered his face and blew in the wind as if it had life of its own. But that wasn't what struck Tommy dumb. With all that hair in the way Tommy could not be sure of it, yet he'd have sworn the man was grinning at him. Tommy didn't like it. He felt that grin was full of a peculiar sort of evil, and it gave Tommy such a queer feeling that he hurriedly turned away without saying a word.

Just at that moment the road made a turn and he saw at the side of it, a little distance ahead, a great stone gateway. Tommy knew from the stationmaster's description that it was the entrance to his friend's place.

He gave a great sigh of relief. 'Pull up!' he cried to the driver. 'This is where I get out.'

But the driver made no sign of stopping, and the horse went racing past the gate. Tommy rose in his seat, shouting, 'Stop!' Just then the cartwheels hit some obstruction in the road and Tommy, taken unawares, lost his balance. Over the side of the cart he flew and landed in the road on his hands and knees. By the time he pulled himself together and got to his feet, the cart was out of sight, although he could still hear the horse's hooves pounding down the other side of the hill.

Tommy would have liked to have had a chance to tell the fellow exactly what he thought of him, but it was too late for that. The cart was gone, and Tommy's bag had gone with it, but at least he hadn't paid the driver. Taking what comfort he could from that, Tommy limped back to the gateway, and up the drive to the door of his friend's house.

Tommy's friend was terribly surprised when he opened the door at Tommy's knock, and saw him standing there on the doorstone. But when he saw the plight Tommy was in he asked no questions. He hurried Tommy up to his room and saw that he had a good hot bath and found him some dry clothes to put on.

When Tommy came downstairs again, warm and dry and feeling a hundred times better, he was so relieved to have arrived safely that he was prepared to treat his whole experience as a joke. He handed over the telegram and told his friend he didn't think much of the telegraph service in the Highlands.

Tommy's friend had several other guests staying with him and they all gathered around Tommy now to hear the story of his mishap.

'Och, Tommy lad,' said his friend. ' 'Tis a long road and a bad night for walking.'

'Did you walk all the way?' asked one of the guests.

'Well, no,' said Tommy. 'But I wish that I had. I got a lift from one of your wild Highlanders. I never had such a ride in my life before and I hope that I never shall again. And to top it all, the fellow went off with my bag.'

'I wonder who it would be?' asked Tommy's friend. 'Not many would be travelling in weather the like of this at night. The road is bad enough at best. A bit of rain makes it terrible.'

'I'll grant you that,' said Tommy. 'The fellow was driving a tilt cart.'

'A tilt cart!' exclaimed another man. 'Och, they're none so common hereabouts. The only one I call to mind is the one belonging to auld Rabbie MacLaren.'

'Now that you mention it, I remember,' said Tommy. 'That was the name of the man the stationmaster told me to have a care for. I suppose he meant that I was to keep out of his way. How I wish I had!'

There was a dead silence for all of five minutes. Then Tommy's friend asked, 'What sort of man was he to look at, Tommy?'

'An old man, I'd say,' Tommy told him. 'He had more hair on his head and face than I've ever seen on a human being before. It probably looked like more than there really was of it, because it was so tangled and matted. Of course it was too dark for me to see much of him.'

'What was the horse like, Tommy?' asked his friend.

'Not what you'd call a big beast,' Tommy answered. 'In fact he was somewhat on the small side. But how he could go! That horse would make a fortune on a race track. We bumped and thumped along at such a pace that I expected both wheels to fly off at any minute.'

''Twas auld Rabbie MacLaren, to be sure!' said the guest who had asked about the tilt cart. 'He was always one to be driving as if the de'il himself was after him. There's a bad spot a mile further on, over the hill. If you miss the road on the turn there, over the cliff you go to the glen below. Auld Rabbie came tearing along hell-bent one stormy night and missed the turn and went over.'

'Went over!' Tommy exclaimed. 'It's a wonder he wasn't killed!'

'Killed?' repeated the other man. 'Of course he was killed. Auld Rabbie's been dead for a dozen years.'

It took Tommy a minute or two to get through his head what he was being told. Then all of a sudden he understood.

'Dead!' screeched Tommy. '*Then I've been riding with a ghost!*' and he fainted dead away.

The next morning one of the gillies brought Tommy's bag up to the house to see if it belonged to anyone there. He'd found it lying in the glen at the foot of the cliff, below the road. It was the good stout sort of bag that is strapped as well as locked, so all the harm that had come to it was a scratch here and there.

Tommy had recovered from his fright by that time, so they took him out and showed him the place where auld Rabbie went over. They told Tommy he was lucky that he left the cart where he did, for when it got to the bad spot the tragedy was always re-enacted and over the cliff again went the old man with his cart and his horse. There had been some folk who got a ride with auld Rabbie, expecting to reach the village over beyond the next hill, who had found themselves below the road in the glen instead. A number of them had been badly hurt, and two or three had never lived to tell the tale.

Tommy suffered no ill effects from his experience. To tell the truth, he was rather proud of it. And as he took his fishing seriously, he didn't let the ride with auld Rabbie spoil his holiday. He stayed on to the end and fished all the streams in the neighbourhood, and had a wonderful time.

But for a long time after he went home to London he couldn't sleep well on stormy nights. As soon as he turned out the light and closed his eyes he started to dream that he was riding wildly over that rough stony road in the tilt cart with the ghost of auld Rabbie MacLaren.

Stories of Fankle the Cat

GEORGE MACKAY BROWN

I: The Dreamer

'Four pounds sugar, pot of raspberry jam, box of matches, "People's Friend", pound tomatoes, six oranges, packet of washing powder,' said Mrs Thomson. 'If there's any change you can buy a bar of chocolate for yourself. I don't know if there'll be any change. Things get dearer and dearer.'

It was a Saturday morning. Mrs Thomson was too busy to go to the store in the village; she had the weekend baking to do. She put two pound notes and the shopping list in the purse and gave the basket and purse to Jenny her daughter.

Outside, the sun shone. There was a sea glitter in the croft kitchen.

'See that he marks the price opposite every item,' said Mrs Thomson. 'Oh dear, I think I'm going to get asthma again. It was that ginger cat prowling about in the yard yesterday – I blame him.'

Jenny was glad to be out in the sun and wind, on the mile-long road to the village. Saturday morning was the most delightful time of the week; well, Friday after tea was almost as good. She whirled around on the road, she swung the shopping basket, the purse leapt into the ditch.

16

'Fancy,' said Jenny, 'if I was to lose the purse! What trouble I would be in! Mam would have asthma all weekend . . .' (Her mother always got asthma when she was worried or annoyed, or if she saw a cat on the garden wall.)

'I'd better behave myself,' said Jenny. 'I will be a quiet gentle girl. I am a young lady living two hundred years ago. I only speak when I'm spoken to. I am modest and good. Soon a gentleman will drive in a coach to my father's estate. He will say, "Sir Jan Thomson, I have long admired, from a distance, your daughter Jenny. I am, as you may have guessed, Sir Algernon Smythe. I am a man of substance and broad acres. May I now respectfully ask for the hand of that charming girl, your daughter?"'

For four hundred yards or so Jenny was a demure eighteenth-century girl. She tripped along modestly, her eyes downcast. It was rash of a young lady, like her, being out on a public road alone. Fancy, if some stranger, to whom she had not been introduced, were to accost her!

'Well, Jenny,' said a deep voice, 'you don't look much like a gangster's moll today, going along so mimsy-mamsy.' (Last Saturday Jenny had been Al Capone's girl-friend.)

It was old Sander Black. His wicked old head peered over the garden wall of Smedhurst at Jenny. He winked a wicked brandy-ball of an eye at Jenny. He wheezed with laughter.

Jenny smiled back. The eighteenth century faded like a Mozartian tune.

Sander Black and Jenny Thomson shared secrets. They lived in worlds unknown to the other islanders: San Francisco, Greenland, a Pacific island, a crystal fortress on the moon.

Sander Black had been a sailor when he was a young man. Then he had come home to run the croft of Smedhurst after the death of his father. He had been retired for five years now; his daughter and son-in-law looked after the fields and animals. He spoke to his daughter and son-in-law, of course, about such things as seed-potatoes and liquid manure; but the treasures of his experience he reserved for Jenny Thomson whenever he chanced to meet her. He remembered rare things for Jenny — how he had skipped ship in Wellington, New Zealand; the

Pacific girl dressed all in flowers he had once been engaged to; the morning he had woken up in a prison hospital in Cadiz, Spain.

He discovered, to his joy, that Jenny had been to places even more remarkable. She had travelled not only in space but in time; she had been in Babylon at the time of Nebuchadnezzar; she had actually been in the theatre in Washington, D.C., on the evening that President Lincoln had been shot!

For a young girl aged eleven, Jenny Thomson had had a remarkable life. Gravely she told her stories, sitting on the grassy verge beside the pipe-smoking old man, Sander Black.

'Well, now,' Sander Black would say, at the conclusion of one of Jenny's rare adventures, 'if that wasn't a most remarkable thing to happen to you, Jenny! . . .' He would smoke in silence for a while. Then he would say, 'Did I tell you about the time I worked in a circus in Baltimore? I was the lion tamer's assistant . . .'

Sometimes a whole Saturday morning would pass in this trading of stories. Then, reluctantly, Jenny would have to drag home, to a drab dinner of such common things as Scotch broth, boiled potatoes, fried haddocks . . .

On this particular Saturday morning, Jenny said, 'I'm sorry, Mr Black, I can't stay and talk to you today. My mam has sent me for messages to the village. I've to hurry, she says. She thinks she's going to have asthma again.'

'No more can I stop and talk to you, Jenny,' said Sander Black. 'I go away today. Off to Leith for six months, maybe more. I'm staying with Albert, my son. Works on the railway. Goodbye, Jenny, I thought I might see you on the road.'

A pang of disappointment went through Jenny. How on earth could she exist without the stories she gave and received every Saturday? The truth is, Jenny was a lonely girl. There was nobody else in the island to share her visions and fantasies with.

'Wait a minute!' cried Jenny. 'We'll have a little talk. Only ten minutes or so.'

But she was speaking to vacancy. The wicked old head had disappeared. Sander's daughter Annabel would be packing his few things into his pasteboard case. In half-an-hour he would be on the ferry-boat, well on the way to Kirkwall and the airport.

She would miss Sander Black!

A desolating thought came to her; it gave her a catch in the breath. Sander Black was old. Supposing he died in Leith, at Albert's house, and was buried with all his treasury of stories; and lay in the grave, his enchanted ear a cold shell!

Jenny was aware of a tear on her cheek. It glittered in the sun. It made a little dark spot in the dust.

'Goodbye, Mr Black,' she whispered.

She walked on towards the village.

She was a young queen – Queen Jenny the Third – whose prime minister, a sage infallible adviser, had been taken from her by a man in a long black coat whose name was Death. How was Queen Jenny to rule over her turbulent kingdom now, with that good old man gone for ever? She walked with slow regal melancholy steps towards the village. How could a young queen like her deal with the bandits in the mountains? The other councillors were young fops – no more than the queen did they know what articles to tax, and how much. Ought she to tax sugar? There had never been a tax on raspberry jam before, or boxes of matches, or newspapers, or fruit and vegetables. The treasury of Queen Jenny might become quite rich, if she were to tax such things. On the other hand, the poor in the cities might starve. There might be a revolution. Oh, how Queen Jenny wished that her prime minister Lord Black was still in the land of the living!

'Certainly, Jenny,' a voice was saying. 'A pound pot of jam, is it? Would your mam be wanting a giant-size packet of washing powder – they come cheaper?'

She was, after all, standing in the richly-odoured gloom of the general merchant's store in the village, and Tom Strynd the merchant was going through the shopping list item by item.

'I don't know,' she said. 'Mam didn't say.'

When the last of the messages was in the shopping basket, and the account settled, and Jenny was eating her bar of chocolate, Tom Strynd said, 'Well, Jenny, and what's new in the island today?'

'Sander Black's going away to Leith for a holiday,' said Jenny. 'He's going to stay with his son. His son Albert works on the railway.'

'A good riddance,' said Tom Strynd. 'It would be a blessing if that old thing were never to come back again.'

Jenny bit her lip. She ought to have rounded on the greedy little shopkeeper in a blaze of rage. (Indeed she would, later, in the solitude of her room, when she re-enacted the whole scene.) But in truth Jenny was a timid girl, who wouldn't say a cross word to a horse-fly that had stung her.

'You've been crying,' said Tom Strynd. 'What was wrong? Did your mam give you a row about something?'

'No, she didn't,' said Jenny.

'Poor Jenny,' said Tom Strynd. 'Now let me see. Would you like to share a secret with me? I'll show you something to cheer you up. Come out into the yard with me, Jenny.'

Jenny followed Tom Strynd out into the yard, leaving her basket of messages on the counter.

Tom Strynd opened the back of his patched rusty van. There, on a sack, reposed a solitary black kitten. It was very young. It blinked smoky-blue eyes, that were full of alarm, wonderment, mischief.

'Is it yours?' Jenny asked. 'I didn't know you had a cat.'

'I don't,' said Tom Strynd.

'Then where did it come from?' said Jenny.

'There's the mystery,' said the general merchant. 'I opened the back of my van three days ago, to get out some bags of potatoes and turnips, and there, in the corner, was *this*.'

'He's beautiful,' said Jenny.

'I don't like cats,' said Tom Strynd. 'I never have done and I never will. Nasty stinking things. What a noise they make sometimes at night, like a troupe of fiddlers gone off their heads!'

'The little sweetheart,' said Jenny. She put out her hand and with the points of her fingers touched the kitten gently. Immediately the kitten responded – it became one breathing trembling purr, it closed its smoky-blue eyes in an excess of delight, it rose and rubbed its jet-black head against Jenny's knuckles.

'I tell you what,' said Tom Strynd, after he had considered for a time. 'I like you, Jenny. Always have done. My folk always got on well with the Thomsons of Inquoy. Ask your father. Well, Jenny, I've grown very fond of this cat in the last day or two. It's going to break my heart to let him go. Funny that, isn't it, especially when I don't fancy cats all that much? But go he'll have to — I just don't have the time to look after him. You know the way it is with kittens, they need to be played with a lot, cuddled and stroked and fed. They have to be trained too. I've been thinking, Jenny. Yes, I spent all last night wondering what to do with this dear little beast. Finally a perfect solution occurred to me — "Jenny Thomson from Inquoy, she's the very girl to own him. She'd look after him well . . ." So, Jenny, he's yours. I'm giving this valuable kitten to you. Pure-bred — I don't need to tell you that. You can see he'll be a good ratter, can't you? Just look at them claws! Have you felt his teeth? Like razors. Every farm on this island would give a lot for a kitten like this. But you know the way some farmers treat their cats — a kick every time they pass them. Coarse brutes! I'm not having anything like that, Jenny, not with this honey of a kitten. So, Jenny, I'm going to pick him up now and give him to you. It'll be a load off my mind . . . Come, kittums, you're going home with Jenny.'

'I'm sorry, Mr Strynd,' said Jenny. 'It's impossible.'

'You'll never see a kitten like this again,' said Tom Strynd.

'I won't,' said Jenny. 'He's simply the loveliest kitten in the whole world.'

'He loves you already,' said Tom Strynd.

'I think so,' said Jenny. 'Oh, I hope so.'

'He's yours then,' said Tom Strynd. 'No trouble. Take him away at once.'

Jenny shook her head. 'My mother would kill me. My mother hates cats. The very thought of them makes her ill.'

'A great pity that,' said Tom Strynd slowly. 'Because, Jenny, do you know what I'll have to do tonight, as soon as I get back in my van from the farms?'

Jenny shook her head again.

The little bell attached to the top of the shop door 'pinged' furiously three times. Tom Strynd had a customer, a customer who needed something urgently, a customer who was beginning to get impatient.

'Coming!' shouted Tom Strynd. 'I'm coming! I can't be everywhere at once!' Then he turned to Jenny and said in a low sweet voice, 'After I get back from the farms, Jenny, I'm going to take this little kitten, Jenny. I'm going to tie a heavy stone round his neck. Then I'm going to drop him in the millpond.'

The little bell pinged again, twice.

Tom Strynd scuttled across the yard towards the shop, crying, 'Patience, patience! Job had patience.'

Jenny lifted the condemned kitten in her arms. She swayed it back and fore. She whispered fiercely, 'He won't! Don't be feared, peedie friend. Not a hair of you will be harmed. You'll never see the millpond, tonight or any other night. I'm Jenny. I'm your friend. You're coming home with me.'

It was only as Jenny rounded the shoulder of the little hill and saw Inquoy below her, its chimney smoking, that she realized the enormity of her deed. Who was she to promise sanctuary to a kitten, even such a beautiful kitten as this? It couldn't be − it was impossible. Her mother was bound to find out in time, no matter how cunningly Jenny hid the animal. Her mother could smell out cats − and the smell of a cat within half-a-mile of Inquoy made her ill with disgust.

'Stop here meantime,' said Jenny to the kitten. 'I'm not leaving you. I'll be back in a minute with some milk and breadcrumbs. You sweetheart.' She kissed the little cold nose of the kitten. She put him into an old disused hen-house and closed the door.

Half-way to the croft-house, Jenny paused. She realized she would need all her imagination to get through the next day or two. She sat down on the wall of the kail-yard. She closed her eyes. She picked up a stone. She said slowly, in a foreign accent, 'I am a spy. I have no name. I have a secret number. I am in enemy territory. If I'm caught I will be killed without mercy. I have been sent here by M.I.5. My task: to rescue a very important prisoner, someone with secrets so precious that all the countries of the earth want desperately to have them. The first part of my mission is accomplished. (M.I.5, can you hear me? This is 527 speaking.) I have had success. I entered the prison today. I shot the guards, I brought the prisoner out safe. All is well. But a worse hazard lies ahead – how to get the prisoner out of the country. Can you hear me, M.I.5? I have concealed the prisoner in a peasant's hut. I will attempt tonight, under cover of darkness, to get the prisoner past the dock and embarkation authorities. It will not be easy. The alarm has been raised. Their anti-espionage people are everywhere. I am sending this radio message from a bleak hillside above the port. I have seen through the binoculars a likely ship. Her name is *Fantasy*. I am returning now, at sunset, to the peasant's hut. You will hear from me once we are safely aboard the ship. If you do not hear from me, then it is all over – the worst has happened – the prisoner and your 527 are captured, probably dead . . .'

A cold voice said at her shoulder, 'What kept you so long?'

Jenny said to her mother, 'Mr Strynd spoke and spoke and spoke.'

'Where are the messages?' said Mrs Thomson.

Jenny had forgotten the messages in the joy and anxiety she had experienced that morning.

'I'm sorry, mam,' she said. 'I don't know what I can have been thinking about. I got the messages all right, and I paid for them. They're safe enough. I just left them, somehow or other, in the shop. I'll go right back at once and get them.'

Such a violent spasm of asthma struck Mrs Thomson then that she had to sit down on the kail-yard wall, five yards away from Jenny. It was four or five minutes before she could speak.

'You foolish ungrateful girl!' said her mother at last. 'What am I to do with you? Does any other woman in this island, or in the whole world, have a daughter like you? I sometimes wonder if you're quite right in the head. A beautiful spy in enemy territory! The Lord give me patience. Who are your enemies, girl – myself and your father? Let me tell you something, Jenny. Let me warn you. If you go on with those stupid dreams and fantasies, you'll come to a bad end! You will, for sure. Listen, girl, I'll tell you exactly who you are. You're Jenny Thomson, aged eleven, of Inquoy farm, in a little island in Orkney. You're a schoolgirl. When you leave school you'll probably work on a farm somewhere. When you're a bit older, if you're lucky, some decent farmer might take you for his wife. Then you'll likely have two or three bairns. Then you'll be an old woman with rheumatics and wrinkles, telling stories beside the fire to grandchildren. That's the way it always will be. Resign yourself to it. It'll save you a lot of unhappiness, Jenny. Whenever you feel those foolish dreams taking hold of you, say to yourself firmly: *No. I'm poor Jenny Thomson, of Inquoy croft.* That'll bring you to your senses . . . I have nothing more to say.'

'Yes, mother,' said Jenny, 'I'm sorry. I'll try not to imagine foolish things again. I'm Jenny, nothing else.'

'You'd better go back and get the messages then,' said Mrs Thomson, 'before somebody steals them.'

Jenny got up from the wall and gave her mother a sorrowful guilty kiss on the cheek.

'My asthma is very bad today,' said Mrs Thomson. 'There's a good girl. We won't say another word about it . . . Worst asthma I've had all summer. There must be some cat or other prowling around.'

Jenny crept off once more in the direction of the village, a plain, chastened, rather stupid croft girl.

'A name,' whispered Jenny. 'What name will I give the cat?' As she passed the smithy she said, '*Fankle* . . . Because, little dear, you have caused so many difficulties already. Your name will be Fankle.'

II: Discovery

'But where can we hide him?' said Jenny to her father. 'Mother's sure to find him, one day or another.'

Jan Thomson pondered. Then he said, 'In the boatshed. Your mother never goes there.'

So Fankle was bedded down in an old fishbox in the boatshed, with a lining of lamb's-wool plucked by Jenny from the barbed wire, to keep him warm.

'Jenny,' said Mrs Thomson the very next afternoon, 'that's twice today you've gone out with a saucer of milk. What's going on?'

'Nothing,' said Jenny. 'There's a starling with a hurt leg in the yard. I'm helping him to stay alive.'

'That's good of you, Jenny,' said her mother.

The little black kitten grew fast in the boatshed, fed on saucers of milk, and on milk-soaked bread, and pieces of fish and chicken. Soon he was scampering all over the boatshed, chasing flies and beetles and pieces of dust in sunshine. Jenny brought him his milk three times a day. Then she would stroke him, and he would purr like a powerful little engine. 'Fankle's a very good singer,' Jenny assured her father.

A terrible thing happened – Mrs Thomson's cheese and butter were being interfered with! Something was plundering these delicious plates in the cupboard every night. (Mrs Thomson was a very good dairy-woman.)

'No mistake,' said Jan Thomson. 'It's a rat – and a big clever one at that.'

So, traps were set here and there about the croft-house, primed with cheese and grilled bacon. But he was a clever rat all right. He only came out at night, and so nobody in the house ever saw him, and he was so diabolically clever he could get the cheese or the bacon out of the trap without springing it.

'Oh dear,' said Mrs Thomson, 'what will we do? If that old dog was any good, he'd catch the thief.'

The fact was that Robbie, the old collie, who had been a very good dog in his day, now slept the remnant of his life away before the fire. If, on one of his chance meanders round the steading, he saw a rat or a mouse or a young rabbit, he gave it a sleepy benevolent look. Robbie's days as a farm-dog were over.

'Whatever can be done?' cried Jenny's mother. 'Do you know

25

this, the rat bit and scratched into a whole pound of sausages in the night. What we were supposed to have for our tea. And the cupboard door was locked!'

Fankle flourished in the boatshed. He loved scuttling among the lobster creels, the oars, and the coiled fishing lines. He was on good terms with the many spiders in the shed, and with the blackbird that came every morning to sing on the roof. But cats love best of all to be outside; Jenny could only give him his liberty when Mrs Thomson was away for the day, shopping in Kirkwall or Hamnavoe. Then Fankle had a wonderful time between the grass and the clouds. He ran among the chickens, who clucked indignantly at him. He even squared up to the cow, sparring and dancing away, like a little David threatening Goliath. Once he even ventured into the house, and spent a companionable hour with Robbie in front of the fire. He licked Robbie's ear, very delicately. Then he got up, stretched himself, and strolled across to examine with great interest a crack in the kitchen floor, where the flagstone had worn.

Fankle sniffed at that fissure for quite a while. He tried to look in. He sniffed again, and gave a little growl in his throat. Then Jenny had to seize him and run with him into the boatshed, for she had heard the sound of a Ford car on the road. Her mother was returning from the ferry-boat.

'Something very strange is going on in this house,' Mrs Thomson complained one morning at breakfast. 'Jenny, what *are* you doing with all that milk, day after day? That bird must have flown away ages ago.'

Jenny assured her that the starling was still hopping around on one leg, and drinking more than ever, but soon now he would be better.

'If I haven't enough to put up with,' said Mrs Thomson, 'with that pirate of a rat! I'm as sure as sure can be that I heard a cat miaowing early this morning, somewhere around the house.'

Her man assured her that that was impossible. There had

never been any cat on that croft since they had got married; he knew how much she hated cats.

But Mrs Thomson caught the guilty look that father and daughter exchanged across the table.

'Stray cat or not,' said Mrs Thomson, 'it won't stay here – I can assure you of that.' Jenny's mother was in a bad mood that morning, because in the night the rat had made a skeleton of the cold chicken they were to have, with salad, for their dinner that day.

Mrs Thomson, one Saturday in June, was to be one of a group of trippers. The island branch of the Women's Rural Institute was going on a sea outing to the island of Hoy.

As soon as Mrs Thomson, in her new floral dress and modish hat, was round the corner and out of sight, Jenny ran and flung open the boatshed door. It seemed as if a little patch of midnight whirled past her into the sun and wind. Fankle was all set to have a riotous day of it. He leapt softly between byre and barn. When Jenny looked again, he had disappeared into the long grass of the meadow.

Jenny went indoors and busied herself about the house. She was the woman in charge that day. She would have to make the beds, keep a flame in the fire, prepare dinner and tea for her dad. Jenny loved doing these jobs.

While Jenny was scrubbing the potatoes in the kitchen sink, queen of the house for a whole day, she glanced through the window and got a terrible shock. There, returning over the hill road, were the lady trippers of the W.R.I. They had only been gone a half hour.

What on earth had happened? Jenny soon learned, once her mother was back home, looking so hurt and downcast. (Poor Mrs Thomson, *everything* seemed to be going wrong for her that summer!)

It transpired that Neil Bell the boatman, who was to have ferried them to Hoy, had suddenly been seized with tummy pains after breakfast, and had been whirled away to hospital in Kirkwall, in a helicopter, with suspected appendicitis. And so the trip was off. 'And this such a lovely day!' complained Mrs Thomson.

She was so disappointed that she had got a headache. 'Never mind,' said Jenny. 'I'm getting on well with the housework. You just sit over there beside the fire, mam, and I'll bring you two aspirins and a cup of tea.'

So Mrs Thomson, looking like one of the hanging gardens of Babylon in her summer dress, sat in the armchair beside the fire, and sighed, and sometimes touched her throbbing temple with delicate fingers.

Meantime Jenny scrubbed the potatoes and dropped them, a cluster of pale globes, into the pot of boiling water. Just then she thought, with sudden panic, about Fankle. Fankle, the forbidden cat, was running about the farm, free as the wind. At any moment Fankle might show his midnight face at the door; and that, on top of everything else, might well prove the end of her poor mother.

Jenny quickly dried her hands on her apron and slid like a shadow through the door.

'Girl, come back!' cried her mother. 'Where do you think you're going? There's the table to set. The potato pot might boil over.'

Jenny returned. She said, rather lamely, that she was going to see if the hens had laid any eggs.

'Plenty of time for that!' said her mother. 'See to the dinner. Your father will be hungry.'

Poor Jenny, she laid the knives and forks on the scrubbed table with a sunken heart. It was a house of gloom and despondency.

'No dinner of course for me,' moaned her mother. 'I couldn't eat a bite.'

Jenny returned one knife and one fork into the table drawer. Then she raised the lid of the ramping potato pot. Right enough, if she had gone out looking for Fankle, the pot would have boiled over, and that would have been another sorrow for her poor mother to bear.

'Jenny,' came the mournful voice from the fireside chair.

'Yes, mother?'

'Open the cupboard. See if that rat was on the rampage last night.'

When Jenny opened the cupboard door, she saw at once that the rat had performed a masterpiece of thieving. He had eluded two cunningly-placed traps. He had approached the large round white cheese that Mrs Thomson had made for the cheese competition at the agricultural show in August. Now, that lovely cheese had been protected by a heavy pyrex dish – it seemed an invulnerable treasure inside a crystal castle. The bandit rat had somehow contrived (who knows how?) to lever up the protective glass, and to make savage inroads into the prize cheese. In fact, the cheese was ruined – you could not have exhibited it at a fair of tramps.

As quietly as she could, Jenny reported the disaster to her mother.

It was more than flesh and blood could bear. Mrs Thomson groaned. Two large tears, like pearls, gathered in her eyes and coursed down her stricken face. She was beyond speech. It was all sighs and groans with her. At last she managed 'doctor', and 'brandy', and 'Why do I have to suffer like this?'; and finally, at the peak of pain, 'That was the loveliest cheese I ever made!'

And she looked at Jenny as if Jenny was personally responsible for all her sufferings.

At this point Jan Thomson came in. The two women of the house poured out to him, in broken phrases, the sum of troubles that had happened. Jan Thomson listened with sympathy (for he was a kind man), and he went over and kissed his wife on the cheek, and stroked her hair, and murmured kind words.

'Now,' said Jenny to herself, 'now is the time to slip away and find that cat and return him to the boatshed!'

But, as it turned out, Jenny did not have to go to that trouble, for Fankle presented himself at the open door – softly, subtly, secretly, a jet black shadow. The cat was carrying across his jaws a creature as big as himself, a long grey sinister shape. The beast was dead. And it was a rat.

As if Fankle knew what was what, he dragged his prey over the flagstone floor and, with the greatest of courtesy, laid the rat at the feet of Mrs Thomson. Then he went over to the other side of the fire, gave his paw a long sweep with his tongue, and began to wash his face. (You have to clean yourself well after a battle with a rat.)

Most ladies, presented with a rat, even a dead rat, would have screamed and gone rushing round the room. Not Mrs Thomson. After a first amazed minute, she fixed the grey shape on the floor with an amazed and satisfied eye. There was no doubt in her mind that here lay the pirate that had ruined the summer for her.

'Good gracious!' cried Jan Thomson in a false voice, 'where on earth did that cat come from? Put him out at once, Jenny. I'll take the rat out to the dunghill.'

'The cat is to remain here, beside the fire,' said Mrs Thomson. 'I like this cat. Isn't he sweet? Isn't he clever? To have killed that demon of a rat! I must say he has a nice kind face. Jenny, this cat, whatever his name is, is to be given a saucer of milk at once.'

'His name is Fankle,' said Jenny.

'Fankle can bide here,' said Mrs Thomson, 'for as long as he likes. He looks as if he belongs here, anyway. Pretty pussy.'

The Consolation Prize

LAVINIA DERWENT

In the days when I was a Mixed Infant at the village school the one and only prize I ever won was for the best dyed egg. The presentation was made by none other than the man who wrote *Peter Pan*, Sir J. M. Barrie, who happened to be staying with friends in the district at the time. It should have been a proud occasion for me, but for one thing. I had not dyed the egg myself.

It was Jessie, the odd-job woman at the farm, who had done the deed for me by covering the egg with a piece of lace and putting an onion (only she called it an ingan) in the water to colour it.

Sir James was greatly impressed and declared that if all eggs looked like mine, he would have a boiled one for his breakfast every morning. To my shame he presented me with a book of Bible stories. There was a picture of the Prodigal Son on the cover, and I ran breathlessly home to present it to Jessie, the rightful winner, but she handed it back to me and said, 'Hoots-toots, lassie, you read it yoursel'. Maybe it'll lairn ye a lesson.'

It did. Next year, to expiate my sins, I did the deed myself. Only better. I found an even lacier piece of lace, put two onions in the water to give it a richer hue, and dyed a couple of eggs to be on the safe side.

Perfect they were, both worthy of first prizes, in my opinion. I swithered about which to take: the rose-patterned one, or the one with wee butterflies on it. It was impossible to choose, so I wrapped them both up in tissue-paper and put them carefully in my schoolbag. Maybe I would get first and second prizes.

I had to stop at the old roadman's cottage, as I did every morning, to collect Wee Wullie. We all have our burdens to bear and Wullie was mine. He was a small shauchly child, with his stockings hanging down and an unwashed, unkempt, neglected look about him. He lived a kind of hand-to-mouth existence with the old roadman, his grandfather, who was often ill and out of work, and seldom, I dare say, had a cooked meal. Though that never occurred to me at the time. I just thought of Wee Wullie as a nuisance. He was always trying to play truant and snivelling, 'I dinna want to be learnt!' But the teacher had told me I must bring him. So I had to act as sergeant-major.

'Come on, you!' I called out at the cottage door; and at last Wee Wullie came shuffling out with his laces trailing from his boots and his patched jersey on back to front. He walked a few paces behind me, like a lord-in-waiting, and I had to turn round every now and again to see that he had not jouked me and done a dash over the fence.

'Where's your dyed egg?' I asked him.

'Haveny got ane,' said Wullie, kicking his toes.

'What?' Fancy not even bothering to dye an egg for the competition! Lazy thing!

Outside Bella-the-Shop's door I had a sudden tussle with myself. After all, I had two eggs.

'Here!' I said, fishing in my schoolbag. 'You can have one of mine.'

I did eenie-meenie-miny-mo and handed him one of the eggs wrapped up in its tissue-paper. I left him clutching it, with his eyes sparkling, and went in to buy a new jotter. I had no money left over to buy sweets; but never mind! It was rumoured that Lady Somebody was coming to judge the dyed eggs and that the first prize would be a big box of chocolates. But what if Wee Wullie won it?

He was still standing where I left him with the tissue-paper clutched in his hand. But where was the egg?

'I've etten't,' he confessed, wiping his mouth.

'Etten't!' I cried, aghast at the enormity of his sin. When I saw bits of coloured shell scattered around him I raged. 'You're a wicked thing! What did you do that for?'

Wee Wullie began to blubber, 'I was h-hungry!'

Hungry! I stared at him in amazement. It had never entered my head that anyone could be so hungry that he would eat a prize-winning dyed egg. It was easy enough for me; the hens just laid them and I went to gather them.

'Stop greetin',' I said crossly. 'Come on; we'll be late.'

I had a fight with myself all the way to the school gate. The bell was ringing before I finally made my great sacrifice.

'Here! Have the other egg,' I said, thrusting it at Wee Wullie. 'But you're not to eat it. It's for the prize.'

Lady Thing was a rotten judge. She gave Maggie Turnbull the box of chocolates, and Wee Wullie was not even in the first three. But at least she gave him a consolation prize. A bar of scented soap. Wee Wullie was as pleased as Punch and sniffed at it all the way home. But it would have been better if he could have 'etten't'.

There and then I decided that I would take an extra dinner-piece with me every day and share it with Wullie. He was still a nuisance, of course; but at least for the next two or three days he smelt of lavender.

Do You Believe in Ghosts?

IAIN CRICHTON SMITH

'I'll tell you something,' said Daial to Iain. 'I believe in ghosts.'

It was Hallowe'en night and they were sitting in Daial's house – which was a thatched one – eating apples and cracking nuts which they had got earlier that evening from the people of the village. It was frosty outside and the night was very calm.

'I don't believe in ghosts,' said Iain, munching an apple. 'You've never seen a ghost, have you?'

'No,' said Daial fiercely, 'but I know people who have. My father saw a ghost at the Corner. It was a woman in a white dress.'

'I don't believe it,' said Iain. 'It was more likely a piece of paper.' And he laughed out loud. 'It was more likely a newspaper. It was the local newspaper.'

'I tell you he did,' said Daial. 'And another thing. They say that if you look between the ears of a horse you will see a ghost. I was told that by my granny.'

'Horses' ears,' said Iain laughing, munching his juicy apple. 'Horses' ears.'

Outside it was very very still, the night was, as it were, entranced under the stars.

'Come on then,' said Daial urgently, as if he had been angered by Iain's dismissive comments. 'We can go and see now. It's

34

eleven o'clock and if there are any ghosts you might see them now. I dare you.'

'All right,' said Iain, throwing the remains of the apple into the fire. 'Come on then.'

And the two of them left the house, shutting the door carefully and noiselessly behind them and entering the calm night with its millions of stars. They could feel their shoes creaking among the frost, and there were little panes of ice on the small pools of water on the road. Daial looked very determined, his chin thrust out as if his honour had been attacked. Iain liked Daial fairly well though Daial hardly read any books and was only interested in fishing and football. Now and again as he walked along he looked up at the sky with its vast city of stars and felt almost dizzy because of its immensity.

'That's the Plough there,' said Iain, 'do you see it? Up there.'

'Who told you that?' said Daial.

'I saw a picture of it in a book. It's shaped like a plough.'

'It's not at all,' said Daial. 'It's not shaped like a plough at all. You never saw a plough like that in your life.'

They were gradually leaving the village now, had in fact passed the last house, and Iain in spite of his earlier protestations was getting a little frightened, for he had heard stories of ghosts at the Corner before. There was one about a sailor home from the Merchant Navy who was supposed to have seen a ghost and after he had rejoined his ship he had fallen from a mast to the deck and had died instantly. People in the village mostly believed in ghosts. They believed that some people had the second sight and could see in advance the body of someone who was about to die though at that particular time he might be walking among them, looking perfectly healthy.

Daial and Iain walked on through the ghostly whiteness of the frost and it seemed to them that the night had turned much colder and also more threatening. There was no noise even of flowing water, for all the streams were locked in frost.

'It's here they see the ghosts,' said Daial in a whisper, his voice trembling a little, perhaps partly with the cold. 'If we had a horse we might see one.'

'Yes,' said Iain still trying to joke, though at the same time he also found himself whispering. 'You could ride the horse and look between its ears.'

The whole earth was a frosty globe, creaking and spectral, and the shine from it was eerie and faint.

'Can you hear anything?' said Daial who was keeping close to Iain.

'No,' said Iain. 'I can't hear anything. There's nothing. We should go back.'

'No,' Daial replied, his teeth chattering. 'W-w-e w-w-on't go back. We have to stay for a while.'

'What would you do if you saw a ghost?' said Iain.

'I would run,' said Daial, 'I would run like hell.'

'I don't know what I would do,' said Iain, and his words seemed to echo through the silent night. 'I might drop dead. Or I might . . .' He suddenly had a terrible thought. Perhaps they were ghosts themselves and the ghost who looked like a ghost to them might be a human being after all. What if a ghost came towards them and then walked through them smiling, and then they suddenly realized that they themselves were ghosts.

'Hey, Daial,' he said, 'what if we are . . .' And then he stopped, for it seemed to him that Daial had turned all white in the frost, that his head and the rest of his body were white, and his legs and shoes were also a shining white. Daial was coming towards him with his mouth open, and where there had been a head there was only a bony skull, its interstices filled with snow. Daial was walking towards him, his hands outstretched, and they were bony without any skin on them. Daial was his enemy, he was a ghost who wished to destroy him, and that was why he had led him out to the Corner to the territory of the ghosts. Daial was not Daial at all, the real Daial was back in the house, and this was a ghost that had taken over Daial's body in order to entice Iain to the place where he was now. Daial was a devil, a corpse.

And suddenly Iain began to run and Daial was running after him. Iain ran crazily with frantic speed but Daial was close on his heels. He was running after him and his white body was blazing with the frost and it seemed to Iain that he was stretching his bony arms towards him. They raced along the cold

36

white road which was so hard that their shoes left no prints on it, and Iain's heart was beating like a hammer, and then they were in the village among the ordinary lights and now they were at Daial's door.

'What happened?' said Daial panting, leaning against the door, his breath coming in huge gasps.

And Iain knew at that moment that this really was Daial, whatever had happened to the other one, and that this one would think of him as a coward for the rest of his life and tell his pals how Iain had run away. And he was even more frightened than he had been before, till he knew what he had to do.

'I saw it,' he said.

'What?' said Daial, his eyes growing round with excitement.

'I saw it,' said Iain again. 'Didn't you see it?'

'What?' said Daial. 'What did you see?'

'I saw it,' said Iain, 'but maybe you don't believe me.'

'What did you see?' said Daial. 'I believe you.'

'It was a coffin,' said Iain. 'I saw a funeral.'

'A funeral?'

'I saw a funeral,' said Iain, 'and there were people in black hats and black coats. You know?'

Daial nodded eagerly.

'And I saw them carrying a coffin,' said Iain, 'and it was all yellow, and it was coming straight for you. You didn't see it. I know you didn't see it. And I saw the coffin open and I saw the face in the coffin.'

'The face?' said Daial and his eyes were fixed on Iain's face, and Iain could hardly hear what he was saying.

'And do you know whose face it was?'

'No,' said Daial breathlessly. 'Whose face was it? Tell me, tell me.'

'It was your face,' said Iain in a high voice. 'It was your face.'

Daial paled.

'But it's all right,' said Iain. 'I saved you. If the coffin doesn't touch you you're all right. I read that in a book. That's why I ran. I knew that you would run after me. And you did. And I saved you. For the coffin would have touched you if I hadn't run.'

'Are you sure,' said Daial, in a frightened trembling voice. 'Are you sure that I'm saved?'

'Yes,' said Iain. 'I saw the edge of the coffin and it was almost touching the patch on your trousers and then I ran.'

'Gosh,' said Daial, 'that's something. You must have the second sight. It almost touched me. Gosh. Wait till I tell the boys tomorrow. You wait.' And then as if it had just occurred to him he said, 'You believe in ghosts now, don't you?'

'Yes, I believe,' said Iain.

'There you are then,' said Daial. 'Gosh. Are you sure if they don't touch you you're all right?'

'Cross my heart,' said Iain.

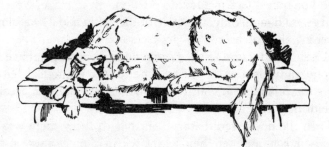

Sandy MacNeil and His Dog

SORCHE NIC LEODHAS

There was once a man named Sandy MacNeil who lived just
outside Cairncraigie. His family in the old days had had plenty
of lands and money, but that was in his great-grandsire's time.
Then the troubled times came along, and when they were over,
his great-grandsire was gone and all the gold and gear had got
themselves lost somehow, too. So all that was handed down to
Sandy were a few starve-crow fields and an old tumble-down
house.

Sandy was never one to mourn for what was gone and long
gone. He made do with what he had and managed to scrape
by on it. Being an easy-going, good-natured sort of a lad, he
wasted no time complaining, and as he went his own gait and
let his neighbours do the same he had plenty of friends and no
enemies worth mentioning. All in all, he was as happy-go-lucky
and contented as if he'd been a laird.

There was one queer thing about Sandy MacNeil. He had a
terrible fancy for dogs, and they had the same for him. He'd be
coming down to the village of a Saturday night, and every tyke
in the place would prick up its ears and wag its tail as he passed
by. Sandy'd go along to the tavern to have a friendly gab
about the news of the week with whoever dropped in, and by
the time he got there, a dozen or maybe more dogs would be

footing it along before and behind him. Each one of them would be trying to shoulder the next one away to get closer to Sandy, and him talking away to them all the while. 'Twas a rare comical thing to see!

When Sandy came to the tavern door, he'd stop, and all the dogs would stop, too. Then Sandy would say polite-like, 'That's all for now, laddies. Be off to your homes, for I cannot ask you in with me.'

Then the dogs would wag their tails to show there was no offence taken, and off they'd go back to their homes, just as Sandy told them to do.

Some folks remarked that it was a queer thing that Sandy MacNeil had no dog of his own. But others would say, why should he, when every other man's dog was just as much his as its master's. Still, the time came when Sandy did get a dog for himself, though the getting of it was no doing of his own.

This is the way it all came about.

One night Sandy was coming home from Cairncraigie. It was past nightfall, for he'd stayed longer than he meant to, the company being good and the talk entertaining. He was swinging along at a fair rate, because the morrow was the Sabbath, and there were jobs that had to be done before midnight came so that he'd not be working on a Sunday.

It was a misty, cloudy sort of a night with a pale moon overhead that gave little light, being mostly behind a cloud. Besides, the road was dark because on either side there were tall hedges that cast their shadows on it. Maybe that's why Sandy didn't notice the dog. He did think once or twice that something was there, but he put it down to a fox or maybe a badger. Being in haste to get home, he paid it no need.

It wasn't till he got to the place where the road met his own lane that he saw it. The hedge stopped there to let the lane through to the road. Just as Sandy got there the moon came peeping out for a minute from under the clouds. That was when he first caught sight of the dog.

Sandy had never seen its like before. The creature looked to be the size of a young calf, and it had long legs and a rough, shaggy coat of fur. From the point of its muzzle to the tip of its tail it was black as coal. The moon went back behind the clouds then, so that was all that Sandy saw of it for the time. But the dog must have had its head turned towards Sandy, because he could see its eyes. The eyes shone with a bright red glow that made Sandy think of the way embers glow under the dead coals when a fire is about to go out.

Sandy was acquainted with all the dogs for miles around, and even from the little he'd seen of this dog he knew that it wasn't one of them. He never thought of being afraid, for he had yet to see the creature that could give him a fright. So he called the dog to come to him. The dog never made a move or a sound. It just stood there with those shining red eyes fixed on Sandy.

'Please yourself!' said Sandy, and he turned into the lane towards his house.

The dog came along with him, keeping to its own side of the road and well away from Sandy. It was plain to see that it had no wish to be friendly. Sandy had great respect for the rights of dogs, as well as of men, so he let it be.

When Sandy got up to his house, the dog was still there. 'Now lad,' said Sandy. ''Tis sure you've come a long way from your home; for if you lived near I'd be knowing you. By that same token, you've a long journey to go before you get home again. You'd best be off and away!'

But the minute Sandy opened the door the dog slipped by him into the house.

'Och now!' cried Sandy. 'Come out o' there, my lad! Where'er you belong, 'tis not here.'

But the dog did not come out and, what with the house so dark and the dog so black, Sandy couldn't see where it was at all.

Sandy went in and found a lamp. He lit it, and then he looked about for the dog. He found it lying on the bench by the fire in the front room. It lay with its nose down on its paws, and its eyes gleaming at Sandy with the same red glow. Now that Sandy could look at it by lamplight, he could see what a huge creature it was. He'd vow it was twice the size of any he'd e'er seen before. But it wasn't its uncommon size that gave

41

Sandy a queer sort of feeling, but something else about it that Sandy couldn't put into words.

However, dogs were dogs, and Sandy was fond of them all. So he said, 'Well then, lie there. Rest yourself a bit if you like. Happen you're weary, poor creature.'

Sandy went about getting things ready for the morn. When he'd finished and filled the kettle and laid out his Sunday clothes, he said coaxingly, 'Come away now, black laddie! 'Tis time for you to be off to where you belong.'

He opened the house door for the dog to go out. The dog made no move to go, but lay still upon the bench. Sandy was used to having dogs do what he told them to do, and it surprised him that this one didn't mind him.

'Happen he's deaf!' he told himself. So he went over to the dog to give it a nudge off the bench. He laid his hand on the dog's shoulder. There was no feeling of flesh or fur under his hand and his fingers came down flat on the bench!

Sandy snatched his hand away as if he'd burnt it. A shiver ran up his spine and back down again. Then he laughed at himself. Half asleep on his feet he must be, and dreaming! It was late and he must be more tired than he'd thought. He went and took the lamp up from the table, carried it over to the fire, and leaned over the bench to take a good look at the dog. He nearly dropped the lamp! He wasn't dreaming! Losh! 'Twas no proper dog there at all! *'Twas the ghost of a dog!*

Sandy backed away. He set the lamp down on the table, his fingers trembling so that it was all he could do to put it upright. Then he sat down to think it over. Of one thing he was sure. He'd not tamper with the creature any further. So the dog lay and looked at Sandy, and Sandy looked at the dog.

What the dog was thinking about a body couldn't tell. At first, Sandy couldn't think at all, but after a while his wits came back to him, and he started to reason the matter out. Ghost or not, the dog appeared to mean him no harm. Sandy told himself that if he were going to be haunted at all he'd rather be haunted by the ghost of a dog than many another he could think of. His great-grandsire, for one, who'd have made a raring ranting old bogle from all that Sandy'd ever heard tell of him. Anyhow, the ghost was there and meant to stay, so what could Sandy do about it? Having come to this conclusion, Sandy told himself that a man needed his rest. So he blew out the lamp and went to bed. And after a while he got off to sleep.

When he woke in the morn he laughed to himself. 'Och!' he said. 'That was a rare fine dream I was having the night's night.' And he went yawning down the stairs to put the kettle over the fire for his morning tea. He looked over at the bench as he passed by the front-room door, just sort of making sure it was a dream.

The dog was still there!

Then and there Sandy made up his mind.

'If I can't drive you out,' he said to the dog, 'neither shall you drive me out. 'Tis my house and I'm staying in it. The place is big enough for the two of us.'

So the dog stayed with Sandy, and Sandy stayed with the dog. At first, Sandy had an eerie feeling seeing it lying there as he came in and out of the house, knowing what it was. But that soon wore off, and he paid it no heed at all. To tell the truth, after a week or two he began to like having it there. It was company for him, living alone as he did.

Except for the night he met it on the road, Sandy never saw it anywhere but on the bench by the fire, although sometimes, as he came up the lane, he had a fancy that it was walking beside him. But when he came into the house, it was always there on the bench.

Sandy never told folk he had a dog, but it wasn't long till they found out for themselves. They found out what sort of a dog it was, too.

One evening, a neighbour of Sandy's stopped by to ask for the loan of some tool or other, and when Sandy stepped out of the house to give it to him, he left the door standing open.

While Sandy stood on the doorstep talking to him, the man – being the sort that is always curious about other folk – peered into the room. He saw the great black dog lying on the bench by the fire.

'Och then!' said the man. 'You've got yourself a dog at last, Sandy MacNeil.'

'Happen I have,' Sandy said.

''Tis an odd-looking creature!' the man exclaimed, leaning to look past Sandy.

'Happen it is,' said Sandy, and he reached behind himself to pull the door to.

The neighbour had a lot more curiosity than he had wits. 'I'll just have a look at it then,' he said, pushing past Sandy into the room.

'I'd not advise it,' Sandy warned him. But the man was already across the room and had his hand on the dog.

The haste with which the man left Sandy's house was amazing. He screeched something at Sandy as he flew past, but what it was Sandy could never tell. Before Sandy could tell him the dog would do him no harm, he was out of sight.

To be sure, the news spread like fire in dry corn stubble. Soon there wasn't anybody that didn't know that Sandy had got a dog for himself that was the ghost of a dog.

It nearly turned the village upside down. Some folk said nothing at all and some said they'd not go near Sandy MacNeil's house for love nor money. But there was an awful sluagh of folk that took it upon themselves to give Sandy a word of advice.

Sandy was used to going his own gait and didn't like being interfered with, so he gave this lot the rough edge of his tongue.

''Tis no concern of yours what kind of dog I've got,' he said angrily.

'Ye'd do well to get rid of it,' they insisted.

'Get rid of it!' Sandy said hotly. 'Och, why should I do that!'

''Tis unnatural, a dog's ghaist,' they said.

'It does no harm,' Sandy insisted.

'Not yet,' said they.

'Nor ever will,' retorted Sandy. 'He suits me fine! Not a penny does he cost me, for he doesn't need to be fed or tended. Nor does he keep folk awake o' nights baying at the moon like the tykes of some folk I could be naming. He can bide with me as long as he likes, so hauld your whisht!'

The truth was that, ghost or no ghost, the dog was Sandy's dog and he'd got terribly fond of it.

What he minded most was that folk wouldn't stop havering about it. It was all they talked about at the tavern and a man could find no comfort there any more. It was just as bad when they met him on the road or in the village. Nobody could find anything to talk about but the big black dog that was a ghost and that was going to bring Sandy terrible bad luck.

One Saturday evening he came home from the village and sat down to take off his boots by the fire. He'd come away extra early, because he couldn't see any sense in staying there because of the way they all kept on at him.

He looked over to the dog and said to it, 'If it's any sort o' luck you're going to bring me, be at it and let's have done with it! Either that or do something to stop their blethering, for I'm weary of hearing them go on about it.'

And being so put out and upset by it all, he did what he'd never have done to a dog had he not been driven to it. He took the boot he had in his hand and hurled it at the dog.

The boot never went near the dog, for which Sandy was glad, because he'd never meant to throw it.

'Och, lad!' said he to the dog. ''Tis sorry I am!'

But the dog looked at him for a minute with its eyes glowing redder than ever, and then it leapt down from the bench and up the stairs. Sandy ran after to see what it was up to, but the dog had too much of a start on him. Just as Sandy got to the top of the stairs the dog gave a great bound that took it right through the wall. Where it went through, it left behind a great hole in the wall, and Sandy ran over to see if he could find out where the dog had gone.

When Sandy got to the hole, he found that it wasn't a hole at all. Instead it was a hidden cupboard that he had never known was there, because it was behind the plaster that had long ago been laid over it. The door of the cupboard stood open now, and while Sandy stood and stared at it a great bag fell off the shelf and dinged down on the floor. The bag flew open, and out poured a great stream of golden coins.

Sandy fell on to his knees before it. 'Luck!' he cried. 'Och, here's all the luck in the world! And 'twas my big black dog that brought it to me!'

It was his great-grandsire's gold that had got itself lost, because he had hidden it away there before he went off to fight in the troubled times. Since he'd got himself killed, he never came back to tell them where it was.

Sandy gathered the gold up into a basket and took it down to the village to show folk the kind of luck the ghost of the big black dog had brought him. The ones who had the most to say before were the very ones who had the least to say when they saw the gold.

The sorry thing for Sandy was that he never saw the dog again, and he missed it sorely. He waited long for it to come back, and there were times he told himself he'd rather have it than all his great-grandsire's gold. But at least he gave up waiting and got himself a tyke to keep him company. It wasn't as big or black or quiet as the other, but it helped.

Now that Sandy was the richest man in the countryside, folk took to calling him The MacNeil, to show their respect. He found himself a bonnie young wife and built himself a fine new house, which he called 'Dog's Luck' just to remind folk where his money came from.

He still goes into the village of a Saturday night, and if you should be there and see a man with a dozen or more dogs footing it along before and behind him, each trying to shoulder the next one out of the way to get closer to him, you'll know that's Sandy MacNeil.

The Kitten

ALEXANDER REID

The feet were tramping directly towards her. In the hot darkness under the tarpaulin the cat cuffed a kitten to silence and listened intently.

She could hear the scruffling and scratching of hens about the straw-littered yard; the muffled grumbling of the turning churn in the dairy; the faint clink and jangle of harness from the stable — drowsy, comfortable, reassuring noises through which the clang of the iron-shod boots on the cobbles broke ominously.

The boots ground to a halt, and three holes in the cover, brilliant, diamond-points of light, went suddenly black. Couching, the cat waited, then sneezed and drew back as the tarpaulin was thrown up and glaring white sunlight struck at her eyes.

She stood over her kittens, the fur of her back bristling and the pupils of her eyes narrowed to pin-points. A kitten mewed plaintively.

For a moment, the hired man stared stupidly at his discovery, then turned towards the stable and called harshly: 'Hi, Maister! Here a wee.'

A second pair of boots clattered across the yard, and the face of the farmer, elderly, dark and taciturn, turned down on the cats.

'So that's whaur she's been,' commented the newcomer slowly.

He bent down to count the kittens and the cat struck at him, scoring a red furrow across the back of his wrist. He caught her by the neck and flung her roughly aside. Mewing she came back and began to lick her kittens. The Master turned away.

'Get rid of them,' he ordered. 'There's ower many cats aboot this place.'

'Aye, Maister,' said the hired man.

Catching the mother he carried her, struggling and swearing, to the stable, flung her in, and latched the door. From the loft he secured an old potato sack and with this in his hand returned to the kittens.

There were five, and he noticed their tigerish markings without comprehending as, one by one, he caught them and thrust them into the bag. They were old enough to struggle, spitting, clawing and biting at his fingers.

Throwing the bag over his shoulder he stumped down the hill to the burn, stopping twice on the way to wipe the sweat that trickled down his face and neck, rising in beads between the roots of his lint-white hair.

Behind him, the buildings of the farm-steading shimmered in the heat. The few trees on the slope raised dry, brittle branches towards a sky bleached almost white. The smell of the farm, mingled with peat-reek, dung, cattle, milk, and the dark tang of the soil, was strong in his nostrils, and when he halted there was no sound but his own breathing and the liquid burbling of the burn.

Throwing the sack on the bank, he stepped into the stream. The water was low, and grasping a great boulder in the bed of the burn he strained to lift it, intending to make a pool.

He felt no reluctance at performing the execution. He had no feelings about the matter. He had drowned kittens before. He would drown them again.

Panting with his exertion, the hired man cupped water between his hands and dashed it over his face and neck in a glistening shower. Then he turned to the sack and its prisoners.

He was in time to catch the second kitten as it struggled out of the bag. Thrusting it back and twisting the mouth of the sack close, he went after the other. Hurrying on the sun-browned grass, treacherous as ice, he slipped and fell headlong, but grasped the runaway in his outflung hand.

It writhed round immediately and sank needle-sharp teeth into his thumb so that he grunted with pain and shook it from him. Unhurt, it fell by a clump of whins and took cover beneath them.

The hired man, his stolidity shaken by frustration, tried to follow. The whins were thick and, scratched for his pains, he drew back, swearing flatly, without colour or passion.

Stooping he could see the eyes of the kitten staring at him from the shadows under the whins. Its back was arched, its fur erect, its mouth open, and its thin lips drawn back over its tiny white teeth.

The hired man saw, again without understanding, the beginnings of tufts on the flattened ears. In his dull mind he felt a dark resentment at this creature which defied him. Rising, he passed his hand up his face in heavy thought, then slithering down to the stream, he began to gather stones. With an armful of small water-washed pebbles he returned to the whins.

First he strove to strike at the kitten from above. The roof of the whins was matted and resilient. The stones could not penetrate it. He flung straight then – to maim or kill – but the angle was difficult and only one missile reached its mark, rebounding from the ground and striking the kitten a glancing blow on the shoulder.

Kneeling, his last stone gone, the hired man watched, the red in his face deepening and thin threads of crimson rising in the whites of his eyes as the blood mounted to his head. A red glow of anger was spreading through his brain. His mouth worked and twisted to an ugly rent.

'Wait – wait,' he cried hoarsely, and, turning, ran heavily up the slope to the trees. He swung his whole weight on a low-hanging branch, snapping it off with a crack like a gun-shot.

Seated on the warm, short turf, the hired man prepared his weapon, paring at the end of the branch till the point was sharp as a dagger. When it was ready he knelt on his left knee and swung the branch to find the balance. The kitten was almost caught.

The savage lance-thrust would have skewered its body as a trout is spiked on the beak of a heron, but the point, slung too low, caught in a fibrous root and snapped off short. Impotently the man jabbed with his broken weapon while the kitten retreated disdainfully to the opposite fringe of the whins.

In the slow-moving mind of the hired man the need to destroy the kitten had become an obsession. Intent on this victim, he forgot the others abandoned by the burn side; forgot the passage of time, and the hard labour of the day behind him. The kitten, in his distorted mind, had grown to a monstrous thing, centring all the frustrations of a brutish existence. He craved to kill . . .

But so far the honours lay with the antagonist.

In a sudden flash of fury the man made a second bodily assault on the whins and a second time retired defeated.

He sat down on the grass to consider the next move as the first breath of the breeze wandered up the hill. As though that were the signal, in the last moments of the sun, a lark rose, close at hand, and mounted the sky on the flood of its own melody.

The man drank in the coolness thankfully, and, taking a pipe from his pocket, lit the embers of tobacco in the bowl. He flung the match from him, still alight, and a dragon's tongue of amber flame ran over the dry grass before the breeze, reached a bare patch of sand and flickered out. Watching it, the hired man knitted his brows and remembered the heather-burning, and mountain hares that ran before the scarlet terror. And he looked at the whins.

The first match blew out in the freshening wind, but at the second the bush burst into crackling flame.

The whins were alight on the leeward side and burned slowly against the wind. Smoke rose thickly, and sparks and lighted shivers of wood sailed off on the wind to light new fires on the grass of the hillside.

Coughing as the pungent smoke entered his lungs, the man

circled the clump till the fire was between him and the farm. He could see the kitten giving ground slowly before the flame. He thought for a moment of lighting this side of the clump also and trapping it between two fires; took his matches from his pocket, hesitated, and replaced them. He could wait.

Slowly, very slowly, the kitten backed towards him. The wind fought for it, delaying, almost holding the advance of the fire through the whins.

Showers of sparks leaped up from the bushes that crackled and spluttered as they burned, but louder than the crackling of the whins, from the farm on the slope of the hill, came another noise – the clamour of voices. The hired man walked clear of the smoke that obscured his view and stared up the hill.

The thatch of the farmhouse, dry as tinder, was aflare.

Gaping, he saw the flames spread to the roof of the byre, to the stables; saw the farmer running the horses to safety, and heard the thunder of hooves as the scared cattle, turned loose, rushed from the yard. He saw a roof collapse in an uprush of smoke and sparks, while a kitten, whose sire was a wild cat, passed out of the whins unnoticed and took refuge in a deserted burrow.

From there, with cold, defiant eyes, it regarded the hired man steadfastly.

Jehovah's Joke

MOLLIE HUNTER

Surprise was more than half the reason for the impact Great-Uncle Archibald first had on our village, for no one there knew that he was a member of the Brethren. Indeed, they had never even heard of the Brethren at that time.

We knew about the Brethren, of course — my sisters, my small brother and myself — for Great-Uncle Archibald was our mother's uncle, and all her family were members of that peculiar band. We knew that the Brethren had meeting-houses instead of churches, and thought that no one except themselves would go to Heaven. They were Saints, according to them, and everyone else was a Sinner. We knew that the fire of the Brethren's hell was stoked very hot for Sinners, but the threat of this had never greatly troubled us, since our knowledge had all been filtered to us through the screen of our mother's gentle nature. Moreover, we had never met Great-Uncle Archibald.

All we knew about him before he decided to move from Edinburgh to our village was that he was seventy-eight years old, and that all his life he had toiled mightily in the Vineyard of the Lord. We accepted this information in prudent silence, and awaited his arrival with a curiosity tempered by our native Scots caution, and also by childhood's automatic distrust of anyone considered to be 'a good example' to us.

The village was more outspoken on the signs that heralded his arrival. These took the form of a sudden rash of religious tracts appearing in letter-boxes, stuck to hedges, or even jammed on to the tines of any garden fork left leaning against its owner's fence; and the message they carried was brief and lurid. All Sinners were damned. The finders, being Sinners, would burn in hell. Therefore, repent — or else!

The villagers, staunch Presbyterians all, were puzzled and resentful, and mother did not mend matters by explaining that the Brethren identified all brands of Christianity different from their own as Anti-Christ.

'It says here,' said Willie Meikle the blacksmith, indignantly reading from a tract he had found impaled on a harrow left for mending outside the smiddy door, 'that I'm a follower o' the Scarlet Woman sittin' on the Beast!'

'Weel, that's neither true nor scriptural,' Dod Thomson the cobbler argued, 'for if ye read the Book o' Revelation aright, ye'll easy see it's the Popish church is the Scarlet Woman sittin' on the Beast.'

'True enough. But there's nane o' us is heathen Papishers, and so there's nae need for a' this damned bigotry,' Meikle announced firmly. And lit his pipe with the tract, to confirm the matter.

All of which, listening in on the men's forum in the smiddy, we heard with some embarrassment, since we knew it was our Great-Aunts Emily and Clara who had left the tracts for the benefit of the village sinners.

We had met the two great-aunts before our first encounter with Great-Uncle Archibald, for they and his daughter Cissie had travelled down from Edinburgh ahead of him to prepare the house for his coming. We quite liked the old dears, and although we thought them a bit dotty we agreed that this was only to be expected, since Clara was seventy-nine and Emily was eighty. Cissie, however, was a different proposition, and her we disliked intensely.

She was forty — or so she claimed, but when Willie Meikle heard this, he said, 'Aye, *and* the rest!' She was tall and skinny. She had yards of straight, straw-coloured hair which she wore wound up over either ear into the huge, circular plaits known as 'earphones', and how she ever heard anything through these was a mystery to us. Her eyes were a watery blue, teamed with pale pink eyelids, and they swam behind the thick, bulging lenses of her spectacles like two tiny blue jellyfish in an aquarium.

It wasn't her appearance we held against her, all the same, for of course we realized she couldn't help that. What we really disliked was the way she behaved, always trying to exchange little confidences with us, which we found *very* embarrassing. She was always so coy, too, and so genteel. She talked about 'lady dogs', and 'daddy pigs', whereas we were country children who spoke quite naturally about 'bitches' and 'boars'. And she was so determinedly *girlish*! She shrieked and fluttered and giggled her way through every conversation, and it made us blush all over to know that every man in the village was laughing behind her back at this.

We got used to Cissie, however. We even went with her to the station to meet Great-Uncle Archibald off the Edinburgh train. We waited there on the platform, a little knot of silent, observant children, with one tall, skinny, talkative woman standing up in the middle of them like a chattering maypole. The train came in and we caught a flash of white from one of the windows trundling past us. It was like a long, white scarf whipping in the wind of the train passing; but Cissie shrieked *'Daddy!'* and hared down the platform after it. That was the first we knew of Great-Uncle Archibald's beard.

We saw the rest of it when he stepped down from the train. It was long. It came down to his navel! It was thick and snowy-white except at the very end, where it sprayed out into a nicotine-yellow fringe, and from the way he stroked and patted it, he was obviously very fond of it.

'Isn't Daddy handsome!' gushed Cissie, hanging on to his arm and gazing adoringly up at his beard.

We were very nearly sick with embarrassment, but worse was to come. We discovered later that she actually used to perch on his knee and *comb* it for him. Cissie confessed this to us with one of her girlish laughs, and a kittenish toss of the head that must have nearly broken her neck — what with the weight of the earphones; but other discoveries about Great-Uncle Archibald were forced on us.

Notably, there was the obvious one that all the other kids in the village called him Santa Claus; and since we could not disown our blood-relationship to him, the joke was on us also. To our shame and horror, too, we found that — far from being content to scatter pious litter over the countryside — Great-Uncle Archibald was determined to smell out sin in the village like a latter-day Matthew Hopkins smelling out witches.

'Brother,' he would boom, stopping gentle and simple alike in their tracks, 'have you seen the Light? Are you Saved? Are you washed in the Blood of the Lamb?'

A stupified 'Eh?' was all the answer he ever got to these unanswerable questions, but this was enough to tell him that here was yet another lost soul waiting to be gathered in; another glorious victory for Jehovah, God of Battles, against the forces of Beelzebub. With beard and forefinger earnestly waggling, he would proceed to expound the Word; and the net result, of course, was that people soon learned to look out for the beard waving down the wind towards them.

The men's forum in the smiddy was adjourned indefinitely. Housewives took to reconnoitring the street before they made a trip to the grocer's shop. But for us, tied by blood as we were to him, there was no escaping Great-Uncle Archibald. Nor was there anyone to stand between us and his determination to put our young lives on a higher, purer plane, for our mother was a widow and more than a little afraid of her terrible uncle.

Lillian was the first to fall foul of him. She was the timid member of the family, poor Lillian, and she met up with Great-Uncle Archibald one evening soon after his arrival in the village when she was off to a rehearsal for a Girl Guide concert.

'Whither away, my child?' the old ogre thundered — genially, for him — through his beard. And Lillian, virtuously aware that only good girls belonged to the Guides, told him whither she was away.

'*Unholy! Ungodly child!*'

They were standing by the little bridge that runs over the

burn by the post office, and his roar of anathema nearly knocked her sideways over the low parapet and into the water. Tearfully, she tried protesting,

'But – it's only the Guides –'

'And there shall be wailing and gnashing of teeth!' the boom of his voice rolled on over her tiny protest. 'The fires shall consume them utterly, and the wicked shall go down into the darkest pit of hell.

'HELL!' he roared at poor, shrinking, eleven-year-old Lillian, pinned right there in the middle of the street for the whole village to witness her shame. 'And you will be there in hell with them, writhing in the flames for your heathenish practices, you wanton, sinful child of Satan. *Girl Guides!* Ha!'

And with a vengeful flourish of the beard, he strode on to tell mother what he thought of her for allowing her girls to join an organization of such abominable worldliness.

My own turn to weather the storm came shortly afterwards when he dropped in to criticize mother's housekeeping and point out to her how extravagant it was to give children jam on their bread, instead of margarine. He caught me on that same occasion, trying on a selection of hats a tinker wouldn't have been seen dead in, but which Cissie had generously donated to mother from her wardrobe. The situation was a natural for a lecture on the sins of the flesh that lead to the Devil, and Great-Uncle Archibald gave me the full treatment.

I was fascinated. I wasn't like Lillian, easily scared; and besides, I was too interested in watching him to listen to what he said. I counted the gold crowns on his teeth when his mouth was wide open for a roar. I watched the bunches of grey hair protruding from each large nostril, and waited in delicious suspense for each snort that set them quivering. I was sure he was enjoying himself, in a way; yet so was I, in my own way, and this did not escape him.

Privately, afterwards, he told mother that he meant to take our religious education properly in hand, starting on the following Sunday, when we would all be bidden to tea at his house.

'Why?' we asked, when mother told us of this invitation.

And she, torn between the truth and the impulse to tease us, said, 'Och, maybe it's his birthday.'

We didn't believe that Great-Uncle Archibald was human enough to have birthdays. But we were obedient children; and so, promptly at 4 p.m. on Sunday, we four girls aged from nine to twelve and our five-year-old brother presented ourselves on his front doorstep. We rang the bell, and from somewhere in the depths of the house Great-Uncle Archibald roared in answer, 'Enter, stranger! Why standest thou without?'

Even Helen, the oldest of us, was startled by this biblical boom. Lillian and little George both looked as if they would cry at the drop of a hymn-book. Elinor, however, was a natural-born mime who had never learned the meaning of fear; and immediately she pulled a face, stuck out her stomach, and stroked an imaginary beard over it. For a nine-year-old it was a splendid imitation of a portly, bearded old gentleman, and we could all have been caught out in the sin of laughter on the Lord's Day if the gentle old great-aunts hadn't saved us by appearing then to open the door for us.

The five little strangers entered, and to their astonishment found a long table set for tea, with – Glory, Hallelujah! – a huge, iced cake as the centre-piece. Instantly – and quite mistakenly, of course – we assumed we had been wrong to doubt that Great-Uncle Archibald was having a birthday, for why otherwise should there be such a shining white masterpiece on the tea table?

This was sound reasoning, so far as we were concerned, for we were a poor family – very poor. Plain fare was all we were accustomed to, and we only got enough of that because mother spent what little money she had on food, and prayed that God would provide something else to buy us shoes and pay the rent. There were seldom any luxuries for us, therefore, and as for birthday cakes –! Even the slices of bread and jam Great-Uncle Archibald had made so much fuss about were only occasional treats, and so we could see no other reason except a birthday for that magnificent cake!

We were fascinated by it; lovingly, greedily fascinated. George was so small that he could just see it over the edge of the table. Lillian, who had a very sweet tooth, positively drooled over it. Elinor rolled her eyes ecstatically, and patted her belly to reassure it of good times coming. I stared as openly as George, but none of the others nudged me as they did him, for they had long ago accepted that I was a born starer at things and people. Helen tried to uphold the dignity of the family by *not* staring, but even she kept jerking her head towards it, as if it had some magnetic power over her. Which it had, course. Which indeed it had!

None of us, as it happened, wished Great-Uncle Archibald a happy birthday. We were too dumbstruck for that, otherwise our mistake would have been uncovered. We had little chance in any case to offer such a wish; for, with a rubbing together and rustling of large, papery palms, Great-Uncle Archibald announced almost immediately, 'Well, we shall have tea, I think.'

We were tablewards like greyhounds out of a trap, but with a solemn uplifting of those large hands he stopped us in our tracks.

'But first, a little hymn of praise to the Almighty.'

'Shall I play, Daddy?'

Cissie minced over to the organ in the corner without needing or waiting for an answer to her empty question. Regretfully we postponed the cake, and made a reluctant group around her.

The little hymn of praise turned out to be a twenty-verse psalm. We sang our way out of the fowler's snare, out of the depths of Israel's woe, and over the River Jordan, and thought the cake was ours — but no! Cissie exchanged the psalm book for the Redemption Hymnal; and, unsophisticated as we were, we noticed the slick way she made the change, and guessed it a well-worn routine of hymns.

There were six of these, finally, not counting that first psalm; and Great-Uncle Archibald gave us no time to recover our wind before he announced, 'And now, a word of prayer at Jehovah's Mercy Seat.'

This was a stumper. In church, like all good Presbyterians, we sat to pray; but the idea of perching on the various chairs scattered around the room, with Great-Uncle Archibald intoning like a ring-master in the middle of a circus, seemed ludicrous to us.

Cissie solved our problem by sliding from her organ-stool, flopping to her knees beside it, and dropping her face down on to her folded hands. We all copied her so far as we were able and within reach of a chair, but I was odd man out, for I was left with only a hassock to kneel beside. I knelt, and still faithfully copying Cissie, tried to put my face in my hands.

I was small, and it was a big hassock; but not all that big. Inevitably, my position resulted in my backside being higher than my head; and yet, having once adopted this peculiar devotional posture, I dared not interrupt Great-Uncle Archibald's prayer by altering it.

It really was too much for Elinor's sense of humour, I suppose, to have to kneel beside her with my face a good foot lower than her own and my backside sticking up in the air just waiting to be pinched. She pinched it, and there were no half-measures with anything Elinor did. I howled. I shot up, straight and indignant, and howled like a banshee.

Great-Uncle Archibald, coming down from the Mercy Seat as rapidly as I had shot up from the hassock, howled also.

'Satan is among us!'

Glaring, he pointed me out for Cissie, the great-aunts and all the family to see. Elinor's eyes silently begged me for pardon, and although I strongly resented being called Satan, I couldn't split on her. Also, this was one time when I was too intimidated to defend myself.

Meekly, backside up-ended again, I endured Great-Uncle Archibald's abjurations, protestations, lamentations and presentations of my supposed repentance to the Almighty. The cake, after all, was still there. For the sake of the cake, I could hold out.

We were dazed by the time it was all over, and stiff with kneeling, yet still our eyes flew to that cake. We took our places at the table, bowed our heads while the Grace was said, and then politely helped to pass the bread and butter and plain scones. There was a long silver knife lying beside the cake, and so we concluded that the cutting was to be done with some ceremony; but this, we thought, was only fitting for so grand an object. Impatiently we waited for Cissie or one of the great-aunts to lift the silver knife, and meanwhile got fuller and fuller of bread and butter.

Each time a great-aunt inquired gently, 'Have you finished, dear?' the one addressed would give a shake of the head; for to have answered 'Yes' to this would have been to imply a refusal of one's share of the cake when it came round. Yet still none of us dared to inquire when it would be, for it had been well dinned into us at home that 'it's manners to wait till you're asked'.

It was only when Great-Uncle Archibald launched into a prayer of thanks to the Almighty 'for the mercies He has so bounteously set before us', that we realized the awful truth. *The cake was not going to be cut at all!* Cakeless we had come, and cakeless we were to be sent home. The injustice, the monstrous swindle of it, took a long time to penetrate, so that we were on the road home before anyone spoke a word. Then it was Helen who said – seeking in a bewildered way to find some sort of reason for it all –

'Well, he's awful old, of course. He probably doesn't know how much children like cake.'

'I bet it was just cardboard – just for show!' Elinor said vindictively.

Quietly, mourningly, Lillian insisted, 'No, it was real. I could *smell* it was real.'

The sensation this conjured up was too much for George. He began to cry. He stopped in the road, and like a small, quivering dog, he lifted his nose to the sky and howled. George was our baby – 'the bairn' to us four girls – and *no one* was permitted to hurt our bairn. We howled in chorus with him, hurling every jeer and insult we could think of in the direction of Great-Uncle Archibald's house.

'We'll get our own back!' we said furiously to mother when we had told her the whole sorry tale. 'We'll get our own back on the old goat-beard!'

'It was my fault to begin with,' she said remorsefully. 'I shouldn't have teased you, girls. But don't you bother trying to get your own back on him. Just you wait, and you'll find the Almighty has a revenge in store that's worse than anything *you* could manage.'

So we waited, planning one wild scheme of vengeance after another, yet still never quite having the courage to carry out these schemes. Not another word would mother tell us either; and so, like the rest of the village, we simply had to grow skilled in dodging Great-Uncle Archibald. When he came in the front door of our house we went out at the back; and in due course, as mother had promised, the Almighty did revenge us.

It was through Cissie that this happened. As mother had long ago discovered, Cissie was secretly in love with a clergyman of the Anglo-Catholic Church, and he (there's no accounting for tastes) returned her love. The time came when Cissie had to reveal all, in order to set a date for her wedding, and Great-Uncle Archibald was shattered to learn that a member of the Brethren – *his daughter!* – proposed to marry a priest of 'the Scarlet Woman'.

Naturally he refused his consent to this unholy union, but Cissie was too infatuated to care whether she got his curse or his blessing. She cast aside her Redemption Hymnal, packed her 'undies', eloped with her clergyman, and married him. Within a year she had a son, and had sent mother a photograph of this baby.

'There,' said mother, showing us the photo. 'There's Great-Uncle Archibald's first grandson – the grandson he's longed for these many years past. But he'll never see the boy, never dandle him on his knee, never pray over him; for Cissie's an outcast in his eyes now, and in his eyes too her bairn was born to damnation. You needn't ask for more revenge than that, children. The old man's mighty sure it's Heaven that waits for him beyond the grave, but that poor silly Cissie was the light of his life, and so he has made a hell for himself, right here on earth.'

When the news got around the village the smiddy forum met in session again and pronounced its verdict.

'He'll not stay here much longer now that there's a disgrace like this been put upon him,' said Dod Thomson the cobbler.

Eckie Morrison, the first ploughman at the Home Farm, said with a deadpan face, 'Aye, it's a terrible thing for a man like him to have his neighbours saying that he's the grandfather o' a bairn born to damnation, as well as father-in-law o' the Scarlet Woman.'

'Sad, though – eh?' said Willie Meikle, hefting his fourteen-pound hammer, and not looking at all sad. 'You'd almost think his old Jehovah was having a joke at his expense!' And crashing hammer to anvil, he rang a triumphant coda to the laughter echoing around the smiddy.

Dod Thomson's forecast proved correct, for Great-Uncle Archibald very soon did go back to living in Edinburgh – so that he could be nearer the Brethren meeting-house, the great aunts told everyone. But be that as it may, the village was certainly allowed to go its way untroubled to damnation from the time his grandson was born to the time of his own departure. Nor did any of us see hide or hair of him again before he died a few months later.

It was in the meeting-house that this happened, in the midst of expounding a text to the Saints; and those who were there at the time, said it was a heart attack that sent his soul winging to the Promised Land. It was also said that the attack had been brought on by a spasm of his continuing rage against Cissie and his misbegotten grandson, for the text he had chosen to expound was,

'They shall cry but there shall be none to help them; yea, even to the Lord they shall cry, but he shall not heed them.'

If there had been an ounce of forgiveness in him, we thought, we might have forgiven him too, now that we had been revenged. But as it was, we got quite a bit of additional satisfaction from the thought of Great-Uncle Archibald arriving in person at the Mercy Seat; and – face to face with Jehovah at last – having to explain about that cake!

Grumphie

F. G. TURNBULL

Since the appearance of Grumphie at the last cattle show at Kirkbracken, pigs have acquired a new significance in that locality. No longer are they regarded merely as potential rashers, but also as creatures of unusual character and temperament.

This state of affairs, however, is due less to the illustrious pig itself than to the tremendous efforts of Tam and Wullie Donaldson, the boys who reared it. Tam and Wullie are the twin sons of the postman, who since the great event has viewed his progeny with mixed feelings of pride and uncertainty. The lads are twelve years old, red-polled, and magnificently freckled.

The affair began when the flooded Ericht river brought Grumphie, then about the size of a rabbit, and sent him whirling half-drowned into a creek where the boys were paddling. Of course they salvaged the pig, and, when its owner could not be traced, claimed the booty.

Sandy Petrie, the farmer of Bannockbrae, offered to provide accommodation for the foundling – an offer which was gladly accepted. And the farmer gave things a send-off when he suggested facetiously that Tam and Wullie should send their pig to the cattle show, due to take place some months later.

Naturally enough, the boys decided that this was a whale of a notion, and they had their own ideas of how a pig should be reared and prepared for prize-winning. As Tam expressed it: 'It has tae be terrible clean an' awfu' fat.' And the fact that Sandy Petrie was to show a pig of his own introduced the competitive touch that inspired the pair to mighty, if unusual, effort.

Operations commenced when the twins arrived at Bannock-brae one Saturday morning bearing a pail, a scrubbing brush, and a piece of perfumed soap wherewith to wash their pig.

Little Grumphie squealed his protest at the first touch of the water; he squirmed and fought, but the twins persisted, although when smothered in suds the pig was as slippery as an eel. However, the victim quietened down quickly and inexplicably, submitting without further struggle to the novel treatment.

After the first application of the brush, Wullie turned to the pail for more water, then he searched about his feet for something.

'Where's the soap?' he asked.

His brother looked around, but the soap had vanished. Presently Tam's inquiring eye lit on Grumphie's face. The little creature was munching busily with a look of supreme bliss on his funny features. White froth dripped from his jaws. Tam crouched to sniff it.

'Great Pete!' he said. 'Lily o' the Valley! The wee beggar's eaten the soap!'

'Hevvins!' gasped Wullie, utterly appalled.

For several moments the twins stared in open-mouthed astonishment, marvelling at the appetite of their pet. Only a few minutes earlier he had had a meal of jawsticker toffee, carrots, potatoes and turnip. But their thoughts were rudely interrupted when Grumphie suddenly uttered a hoarse squeak of dismay and became violently sick.

Somewhat chastened by this experience, Grumphie had not the heart or energy to struggle as his toilet was completed. Then Tam began to collect the washing material. Once more he searched about his feet, then he asked abruptly: 'Where's the brush!'

Instantly Wullie's eyes turned in consternation on Grumphie.

'Hevvins!' he again exclaimed. 'Dinna tell me he's eaten *it*! That's apple, spuds, carrots, turnip, jawsticker, soap, an' now a scrubbin' brush. Gosh! What a stummick!'

But to their intense relief the boys found the brush jammed in the underside of the pail.

As the weeks went by heaven on earth was Grumphie's lot. He was stuffed with foods of every description, and attention such as no pig had ever known before was lavished on him. Wullie attended to his feeding and sty, while Tam attended to his toilet.

Tam's especial pride was Grumphie's peerless tail. It was an absolute gem, he thought — the curliest a pig ever wore. The tuft of pale yellow hair on the end of it was washed, brushed and combed regularly, and encouraged by such solicitude it lengthened considerably. But the soap had to be chosen with discretion. The perfumed variety was hopeless, it possessed such a fascination for the pig. So eager was he to eat it, the twins dared not put it down within his reach. As a substitute they tried carbolic, and Grumphie's interest in the soap immediately waned.

Later, as his weight and strength increased, the pig began to assert his independence. He accepted his mighty meals as his birthright, but he began to take exception to the washing. Whereupon he developed a fraction of his lazy brain to deal with the situation, and kicked the water pail over whenever he saw it. When the lads countered this move by placing the pail on the low sty roof, Grumphie refused to stand still; he raced screeching round the sty with the twins and the brush in pursuit.

'Och, this'll no' dae!' panted Wullie one morning after a strenuous and vain pursuit. 'We'll have to tie him up.'

Tam agreed. 'I'll tell ye,' he said. 'Let's shove his tail through yon wee hole in that board an' tie a knot on the other side.'

After a herculean struggle the twins managed to poke Grumphie's tail through the hole, but found that the thing would not tie in a knot. So a piece of thin rope was attached to it by a cunning hitch, and a stone on the other end of the rope anchored the rebellious porker securely to the sty wall. He uttered blood-curdling shrieks and pulled with all his might, but the rope would not break, nor would his tail tear out at the roots.

The washing proceeded, and when the pig received his final wipe down the rope was removed. With a surly grunt of relief Grumphie waddled towards his food trough, and as he did so a look of horror overspread the faces of the twins. They stared as though hypnotized at the stern of their pig.

In his struggle to escape he had straightened his tail. Gone was the curl that had delighted the hearts of his owners. The appendage stuck out and upwards, stiff as a poker, whilst the drooping pennant of hair at the end accentuated its oddity. Tam was on the verge of tears.

'Look,' he said. 'After a' my brushin' an' combin', we've gone an' took the spring oot o' it.'

'Ay,' added Wullie, gloomily, 'an' a pig withoot a curly tail is as much use at a show as a hedgehog is in your bed. That's done it noo.'

But having gone so far with the preparation of their pet, the lads could not let a straightened tail baulk them of a possible prize. Presuming that the sinews were strained, they borrowed some embrocation from Sandy Petrie and proceeded to anoint Grumphie's rudder. They rubbed and rubbed, letting the tail go now and then to see whether it would assume its earlier curl. But no. It remained as stiff as ever, without the least suspicion of a twist.

The treatment was repeated at intervals for a week, without success. In desperation Tam suggested that they thread the tail through a coiled length of lead gas pipe. The pipe was obtained and the stubborn tail pulled through it with a string, then the whole spectacular arrangement was firmly fastened to Grumphie's rear.

Three days later, with bated breath, the boys removed the pipe, screwing it off carefully so that a possible new curl might not be disturbed. But the confounded thing seemed straighter than ever. It was then coiled round and round a thin stick and tightly bound with string. This device also failed in its object, and the heartbroken twins concluded that the glory had departed for ever from the plumpest end of Grumphie.

While they sat and stared despondently at the pig a large blue fly whizzed round and round, then lit on Grumphie's back. Wullie flicked it away and scratched the spot where it had landed. And to the unbounded delight and astonishment of the boys, the obstinate tail slowly but surely assumed its normal curl.

For a long, breathless moment Tam and Wullie gazed popeyed at the miracle, then, throwing himself on his knees beside the pig, Tam looked with moist affection into Grumphie's bleary eyes and said:

'Weel, noo; there's a real, clever auld beast. Ye deserve a —' His voice trailed away in dismay. That brute of a tail had gone and straightened out again.

Wullie wondered if the scratching, which Grumphie had always enjoyed, had anything to do with it. Again he rubbed his fingers along the rough hide, and in immediate response the tail curled up once more. He ceased rubbing, and the tail poked out again. This was terrific. The next five minutes were spent in intermittent scratchings and hilarious laughter as the remarkable tail popped out and in.

'By gosh, this is something like a pig!' said Tam with enthusiasm. 'All we have tae do tae mak' him curl his tail at the show is just tae scratch his back. Hooray, we'll get a prize wi' him yet!'

The evening before the show was an awful experience for Grumphie. He was scrubbed and scoured until he was almost skinned. Then to ease his hurt feelings he was given the mightiest meal of all. Here was consolation. Life, he felt, still had its points.

While he devoured his food, Tam seated himself in the rear to devote his attention to the hair on the porker's tail. He teased it out, brushed it tenderly, then applied brilliantine and screwed it up in a curling-pin. The captivating odour of the dressing wafted to Grumphie's nose. He sniffed, and traced it to its source, but was much too fat to bend far in the middle, and so was denied the privilege of a chew at his own tail. Life lost a point.

While the pig cleaned the corners of his trough, his proud owners wondered if there was anything further they could do to enhance his appearance. Tam studied the toe of his boot while considering, and there he found inspiration.

'Wullie!' he exclaimed. 'What about blackenin' his trotters wi' boot polish. They'd show up a lot better than they dae noo.'

'Great idea,' agreed Wullie. 'We'll dae just that. An' Mr Petrie says we can get a cart specially for him in the mornin', so we'll tie him up in paper tae keep him clean on the road.'

The twins arrived at the show next day in a downpour of rain. The judges had decided that in view of the weather all those animals that could walk should be brought into the ring under cover for judging. So the twins left Grumphie in the cart with a cover to keep him dry until it was his turn to appear, and they went inside to witness the parade of animals.

The ring where the judging took place was surrounded by tiers of seats where farmers and their friends sat discussing and criticizing the entries. With them sat Tam and Wullie, until it was announced that the pigs would now come in. They waited near the door to hear their number called. It was 23 — the last on the list. In the interval Sandy Petrie had spoken to the judges, warning them that the final exhibit was something of a novelty, and he related its history.

When the second last number was reached the twins dashed out and unwrapped their pet. Wullie brushed his bristles until they shone, and Tam removed the curling-pin from his tail. They were polishing his blackened feet with their handkerchiefs when a raucous voice bawled: 'Number Twenty-three.'

'Come on; oot wi' ye!' urged the lads excitedly. With a grunt of relief the pig leapt heavily from the cart, and guiding him carefully, the twins drove him towards the ring. At every other step they glanced at his tail. It was tightly curled. There was a toffee apple in his mouth. Then into the ring marched the postman's sons and their pig.

A murmur of surprise and amusement arose from the assembled farmers as the trio came in. This was followed by a ripple of laughter when the black trotters were noticed, and the beautifully waved tail. The boys blushed furiously.

'Umph!'

Grumphie uttered a grunt of disapproval. Apparently he disliked noisy crowds, and to express his feelings he unwound his tail and stuck it straight out. A gale of laughter greeted this feat, but it was nothing to the roar of approval that arose when Tam, with a look of desperation, seized the offending object and tried to curl it up again.

With the pig in his present humour it was like trying to put a curl in rubber. The thing sprang out straight immediately the boy released it. At this the audience was convulsed with mirth.

Seeing the state of affairs, Wullie began to scratch the pig's thick neck energetically with one hand and to stroke the underside of his fat tummy with the other. Rummaging frantically in his pocket, Tam produced another toffee apple and rammed it into the sulky porker's mouth.

By a storm of hand-clapping the farmers showed their appreciation of this cunning move. But Grumphie refused to respond. He wanted to get out of here, and no amount of scratching or toffee would make him curl his rudder if he didn't want to.

Meanwhile Tam wrought manfully. Now and again when he had pushed it in, the tail would remain coiled for an instant. And, watching it like a hawk, he knelt with upheld hands ready to push it in again should the infernal thing shoot out.

The judges leaned against the railing and howled. Never in all their lives had they seen anything like this. The pig was almost hidden from sight by the boys who tried so desperately to make it happy. The farmers roared with delight; tears of joy streamed down their weather-beaten faces. They hadn't enjoyed anything so much since the day when a stallion bit the judge's ear off.

The officials held a quick consultation, then the leading judge stifled his laughter and addressed the boys.

'If only your pig had a permanent curl in his tail,' he said, 'he would have got a prize. He's a magnificent specimen except for that one flaw.'

The twins looked at each other in despair. Then suddenly Tam bawled:

'Wullie; bolt oot an' get a cake o' scented soap.'

A tremendous yell from the audience followed this extraordinary command, and a loud cheer accompanied Wullie's exit.

'If yer honors'll wait just one wee minnit,' said Tam pleadingly to the judges, 'we'll put a better curl in Grumphie's tail than ye ever saw before.'

Hearing Tam's plea, the judges looked inquiringly at one another and nodded.

Three minutes later Wullie dashed into the ring, tearing the wrapping from a tablet of highly perfumed soap. He flopped down on his knees in front of the disgruntled animal and held out the offering.

'Here; eat it, ye stubborn brute,' he growled savagely.

'Now then, Grumphie,' wheedled Tam, 'ye're a fine pig. Will ye no' curl your bonny tail up? I'll feed ye on jawsticker and scented soap as lang as ye live if ye dae.'

Grumphie sniffed the Lily of the Valley, then with a grunt of pleasure he opened his mouth and engulfed the titbit. And now the show, prizes, competition and everything else were forgotten as every eye focused on Grumphie's tail. Slowly it began to bend, then with a gay whirl it assumed the tightest curl that ever adorned the blunt end of a pig.

The result was pandemonium. Cheer upon cheer rang out, and wild, insistent cries of 'Special! Special! Special!' And in response to the general demand the judges decided to award the twins a special prize for their remarkable pig. A fresh burst of cheering greeted the announcement, and with freckled, beaming faces the boys looked up to the audience.

The leading judge called to his clerk for a 'special' ticket, and the gaily coloured card was handed to him. In honour of the occasion the official determined to add a longer length of string and hang the card round Grumphie's neck himself. Down he crouched before the pig and reached out his hands to fasten the string round the fat neck.

Suddenly Grumphie emitted a queer, gurgling sound: 'Uuuumph, grumph, aaaouwp!' Tam and Wullie danced on their toes, yelling frantically.

Grumphie

'Look oot, yer honour: *he's goin' tae be sick!'*

The next instant Grumphie proved it, and in a mighty bound the judge hurled himself to the railings out of the way. Twenty seconds later, helpless with mirth, the audience saw Grumphie pick up his prize card and devour it with every sign of satisfaction. And in a resounding thunder of applause, Tam and Wullie drove Grumphie out of the ring.

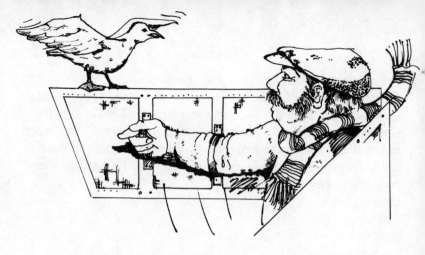

Icarus

GEORGE MACKAY BROWN

There are some folk who take a great delight in prophesying the end of the world. It is a kind of hobby with them. They sit around with pencils and bits of paper, and they work out, by manipulating some of the obscure symbols and figures in Revelation, the very day and hour when doom will fall. They've never brought it off yet, but they keep on trying.

My Uncle Tom is one of those people. 'Old Apocalypse' they call him in the smithy. So it was no surprise to me when two Sundays ago, he whispered in my ear: 'Thursday, ten past two in the afternoon.' We had spent a very pleasant evening round the fire, talking about shipwrecks and tinkers and storms. Aunt Bella's ale had been in splendid condition. Finally, towards midnight, I had risen to go home, and suddenly all the laughter went out of Tom and he said: 'Thursday, ten past two in the afternoon.' Bella clucked disapprovingly in the background. She doesn't hold with all that nonsense.

No more do I, and I forgot all about it till the Wednesday evening, when I called along at their croft with a few haddocks I had caught off Hoy that afternoon. Bella herded me into the straw chair beside the fire and put a bowl of ale in my hands. While she gutted the fish she told me, in one riotous spate of gossip, what couples were getting married and what girls were having babies and what boys had got summonses for running their bikes without a licence.

'Where's Tom?' I said.

The last haddock tail went flying from her scissors. 'He's out in the shed,' she said sharply, 'making ready for Thursday.'

I wandered out to the shed. I didn't go in, for when the prophetic mood is on my Uncle Tom he's no fun at all. I looked through the window, and there he was working on the weirdest contraption that ever was. The bench was piled with a complication of wood and canvas and leather straps and Tom was hammering away at it furiously. I never saw anything quite like it.

I went back into the kitchen to finish my ale.

'What's he making?' I asked Bella.

'Wings,' she said. 'The old fool.'

Then she got on to talking about her favourite subjects – Jo Grimond and the local strathspey society. She was a lot more cheerful by the time I left.

The next day, Thursday, was the Dounby Show. If you've never been to the Dounby Show you've missed one of the wonders of the north. All the nine parishes meet together that day in two small fields beside the village. All the beauty and splendour of their livestock are on show – proud ponderous Clydesdales, bulls like black cubes (oh, the majesty and stupidity of their curled brows!), sheep with mild snowy fleeces, caged cockerels giving the sun a raging salute every five minutes. Among them wander the laird with his deerstalker and shooting-stick, and Sam the tinker, and everyone in between. Besides, the showmen from the south are there, with their shooting stalls and swingboats and coconut shies. The one little pub in the village is crammed to the doors, and the overflow congregate in the huge gloom of the marquee.

I was having my fortune told by a draped woman who called herself 'Madame Roberta, the World's Greatest Palmist', when it suddenly struck me that this was the afternoon that the world was to end. Today, at ten past two, *Finis* was to be scrawled in brimstone under the long rambling incoherent tragic comic fiction of man's life on earth. I looked at my watch. The time was half-past two.

Uncle Tom was wrong again.

'And I see that you've had one or two wee disappointments,' went on Madame Roberta in her Aberdeen accent. 'But you've got over them. You're going to have a good harvest. That last cow you bought is going to have *three* calves.'

I didn't have the heart to tell her I was a fisherman.

Madame Roberta's voice sank to a whispered chant. 'I see a girl,' she said, 'a tall beautiful girl with fair hair. Give me another two bob and I'll tell you all about her . . .'

The prophets are not doing so well today, I thought, as I emerged from the fortune-telling booth into the full glare and blare of the show. But Madame Roberta is less wrong than Old Apocalypse down there beside the loch.

For life goes on.

That evening, when inn and marquee closed and the last drunkard went home under the moon, I cycled to the croft to see how Uncle Tom was taking his latest disappointment.

The first thing I saw when I turned in at the gate was the contraption, the wing machine. It was lying on the grass like a strange discarded chrysalis.

Aunt Bella was knitting beside the fire.

'What like was the show?' she said.

'Splendid,' I said. 'The best I ever saw.'

Actually it was a pretty ordinary show but when I have the tang of ale on my palate I tend to exaggerate.

'Where's Tom?' I said.

'The ambulance took him away to the hospital an hour ago,' she said mildly. 'He broke his leg.'

And then, while a grey sock grew out of her clicking needles and her spectacles glinted in the firelight, she unfolded the story. The wings, of course, had been for Tom to fly into the sky. It had taken Bella most of the morning to get him harnessed. Then, during dinner (the last meal anybody would ever eat on this earth, he assured her), Tom had decided that he would get a better take-off from the roof. It had taken a great deal of pushing and shoving to get him on to the thatch. The neighbours had come out to see the spectacle, and that had made Bella 'black affronted'. It was all right

74

when he used to sit quietly in the ben room waiting for the trump to blow.

The minutes ticked away. Tom kept looking at his watch. People going to the show stopped to gape at this free spectacle. A trout fisher on the loch looked up with suspended oars. A seagull lighted for a moment on the canvas tip of Tom's right wing. There was complete silence for a few minutes on the hillside.

'Are you down there, Bella?' said Tom at last.

'Yes,' she said, 'I'm here.'

'Would you go in and see what time it is on the alarm clock? My watch says *twelve* minutes past two . . .' Bella could have sworn he was crying just then.

She came out again and said: 'It's fourteen and a half minutes past two.'

Thereupon Tom had his moment of splendid rebellion. He stood erect on the thatch and spread his wings. Then he gave a loud cry and launched himself on the afternoon; and, a presumptuous Icarus, fell beside the peat stack in a wild disorder of legs and canvas and outraged fluttering hens.

Bella left him lying where he was and went across the road to phone for the doctor.

I visited Uncle Tom in hospital last Sunday. He was very cheerful. He spoke about past Dounby Shows and about a darkie who had once come there when he was a boy. This darkie had lain down naked on a bed of nails with three ploughmen standing on him. Afterwards he had licked a red-hot poker, and said 'Sugar!' rolling his eyes round the crowd.

I spent a very pleasant hour with him. Only when I was leaving I noticed, on top of his locker, a small bible open at Revelation, and a piece of paper with calculations scrawled all over it.

'You're still at it,' I said.

'Nineteen sixty-five,' he said, 'June the twenty-fourth. Only I can't make out yet whether it'll be five past four in the morning or ten to eight at night.'

Apart from that, he's getting along as well as can be expected.

Tartan

GEORGE MACKAY BROWN

They anchored the *Eagle* off the rock, in shallow water, between the horns of a white sandy bay. It was a windy morning. Behind the bay stretched a valley of fertile farms.

'We will visit those houses,' said Arnor the helmsman. Olaf who was the skipper that voyage said he would bide on the ship. He had a poem to make about rounding Cape Wrath that would keep him busy.

Four of the Vikings – Arnor, Havard, Kol, Sven – waded ashore. They carried axes in their belts.

Gulls rose from the crag, circled, leaned away to the west.

The first house they came to was empty. But the door stood open. There was a shirt drying on the grass and a dog ran round them in wild noisy circles. Two sheep were tethered near the back wall.

'We will take the sheep as we return,' said Havard.

Between this house and the next house was a small burn running fast and turbid after the recent rain. One by one they leapt across it. Kol did not quite make the far bank and got his feet wet. 'No doubt somebody will pay for this,' he said.

'That was an unlucky thing to happen,' said Sven. 'Everything Kol has done this voyage has been wrong.'

Another dog came at them silently from behind, a tooth

76

grazed Arnor's thigh. Arnor's axe bit the dog to the backbone. The animal howled twice and died where he lay.

In the second house they found a fire burning and a pot of broth hanging over it by a hook. 'This smell makes my nostrils twitch,' said Sven. 'I am sick of the salted beef and raw fish that we eat on board the *Eagle*.'

They sat round the table and put the pot of soup in the centre. While they were supping it Sven raised his head and saw a girl with black hair and black eyes looking at them from the open door. He got to his feet, but by the time he reached the door the girl was three fields away.

They finished the pot of broth. 'I burnt my mouth,' said Kol.

There were some fine woollen blankets in a chest under the bed. 'Set them out,' said Arnor, 'they'll keep us warm at night on the sea.'

'They are not drinking people in this valley,' said Havard, who was turning everything upside down looking for ale.

They crossed a field to the third house, a hovel. From the door they heard muttering and sighing inside. 'There's breath in this house,' said Kol. He leapt into the middle of the floor with a loud berserk yell, but it might have been a fly buzzing in the window for all the attention the old woman paid to him. 'Ah,' she was singing over the sheeted dead child on the bed, 'I thought to see you a shepherd on Morven, or maybe a fisherman poaching salmon at the mouth of the Naver. Or maybe you would be a man with lucky acres and the people would come from far and near to buy your corn. Or you might have been a holy priest at the seven altars of the west.'

· There was a candle burning at the child's head and a cross lay on his breast, tangled in his cold fingers.

Arnor, Havard, and Sven crossed themselves in the door. Kol slunk out like an old dog.

They took nothing from that house but trudged uphill to a neat grey house built into the sheer brae.

At the cairn across the valley, a mile away, a group of plaided men stood watching them.

At the fourth door a voice called to them to come in. A thin man was standing beside a loom with a half-made web in it.

'Strangers from the sea,' he said, 'you are welcome. You have the salt in your throats and I ask you to accept ale from Malcolm the weaver.'

They stood round the door and Malcolm the weaver poured horns of ale for each of them.

'This is passable ale,' said Havard. 'If it had been sour, Malcolm the weaver, we would have stretched you alive on your loom. We would have woven the thread of eternity through you.'

Malcolm the weaver laughed.

'What is the name of this place?' said Arnor.

'It is called Durness,' said Malcolm the weaver. 'They are good people here, except for the man who lives in the tall house beyond the cairn. His name is Duncan, and he will not pay me for the cloth I wove for him last winter, so that he and his wife and his snovelly-nosed children could have coats when the snow came.'

'On account of the average quality of your ale, we will settle matters with this Duncan,' said Arnor. 'Now we need our cups filled again.'

They stayed at Malcolm the weaver's house for an hour or more, and when they got up to go Kol staggered against the door. 'Doubtless somebody will pay for this,' he said thickly.

They took with them a web of cloth without asking leave of Malcolm. It was a grey cloth of fine quality and it had a thick green stripe and a thin brown stripe cutting across it horizontally. It was the kind of Celtic weave they call tartan.

'Take it, take it by all means,' said Malcolm the weaver.

'We were going to take it in any case,' said Sven.

'Tell us,' said Havard from the door, 'who is the girl in Durness with black hair and black eyes and a cleft chin?'

'Her name is Morag,' said Malcolm the weaver, 'and she is the wife of John the shepherd. John has been on the hill all week with the new lambs. I think she is lonely.'

'She makes good soup,' said Arnor. 'And if I could get hold of her for an hour I would cure her loneliness.'

It took them some time to get to the house of Duncan because they had to support Kol who was drunk. Finally they stretched him out along the lee wall of the house. 'A great many people will suffer,' said Kol, and began to snore.

The Gaelic men were still standing beside the cairn, a good distance off, and now the girl with black hair had joined them. They watched the three Vikings going in at the fifth door.

In Duncan's house were three half-grown children, two boys and a girl. 'Where is the purchaser of coats?' said Havard. 'Where is the ruination of poor weavers? Where is Duncan your father?'

'When the Viking ship came into the bay,' said a boy with fair hair, the oldest of the children, 'he took the mare from the stable and put our mother behind him on the mare's back and rode off south to visit his cousin Donald in Lairg.'

'What will you three do when we burn this house down?' said Arnor.

'We will stand outside,' said the boy, 'and we will be warm first and afterwards we will be cold.'

'And when we take away the coats for which Malcolm the weaver has not been paid?' said Arnor.

'Then we will be colder than ever,' said the boy.

'It is a clever child,' said Sven, 'that will doubtless utter much wisdom in the councils of Caithness in a few years' time. Such an orator should not go cold in his youth.'

They gave the children a silver Byzantine coin from their crusade the previous summer and left the house.

They found Kol where they had left him, at the wall, but he was dead. Someone had cut his throat with a corn-hook.

'Now we should destroy the valley,' said Havard.

'No,' said Arnor, 'for I'm heavy with the weaver's drink and it's getting dark and I don't want sickles in my beard. And besides all that the world is well rid of a fool.'

They walked down to the house where the sheep were tethered. Now eight dark figures, including Malcolm the weaver and Morag and the clever-tongued boy (Duncan's son), followed them all the way, keeping to the other side of the ridge. The men were armed with knives and sickles and hay-forks. The moon was beginning to rise over the Caithness hills.

They killed the two sheep and carried them down the beach

on their backs. The full moon was opening and shutting on the sea like the Chinese silk-and-ivory fan that Sven had brought home from Byzantium.

They had a good deal of trouble getting those awkward burdens of wool and mutton on board the *Eagle*.

'Where is Kol?' said Olaf the skipper.

'In a ditch with his throat cut,' said Sven. 'He was fortunate in that he died drunk.'

The Durness people stood silent on the beach, a score of them, and the old bereaved woman raised her hand against them in silent malediction.

The sail fluttered and the blades dipped and rose through lucent musical rings.

'The poem has two good lines out of seven,' said Olaf. 'I will work on it when I get home to Rousay.'

He steered the *Eagle* into the Pentland Firth.

Off Stroma he said, 'The tartan will go to Ingerd in Westray. Kol kept her a tattered trull all her days, but with this cloth she will be a stylish widow for a winter or two.'

Three Fingers Are Plenty

NEIL PATERSON

When I was a child I was dominated by a boy I shall call Kirk. I was brought up in a proud old town on the Moray Firth coast of Scotland, and I was brought up in the North Scottish Presbyterian way, that is, Very Properly Indeed. I have never really understood, therefore, why I was allowed to make a friend of Kirk, for Kirk was far from proper. He was a kind of Scotch Huckleberry Finn – a boy who went barefoot, wore orra patched breeks, smoked a clay cutty, chewed plug tobacco, jeuked the school. By all the standards of our time and place, Kirk was beyond the pale. He even worked on Sundays.

Kirk lived with Baggie McLaughlin and his hairy old wife in the cottage at the foot of our hill. Baggie was a small wizened man who touched his forelock to everyone, even me aged eight, and always walked on the grass verge of the road. He called himself a pig-sticker. He went round the outlying crofts at Martinmas, killing off the pigs at a shilling a time, and this was the only work he ever admitted to. In fact, he was a beachcomber. Kirk used sometimes to say that he was a retired pirate, but I knew quite well that this was an exaggeration. Baggie would not have said boo to a gosling.

His wife was very old. I suppose she must have been about the same age as Baggie, but she looked much older. She was crippled with arthritis, bent like a right angle, and heavily bearded. She rose late and retired early, and when she wanted to go to bed she would hobble to the cottage door and ring a big ship's bell that Baggie had picked off the shore, and then Kirk had to run home and help get her into bed. He said it was a hell of a job getting her into bed, and I bet it was, for she was solid as teak and must have weighed close on sixteen stone.

As far as anybody knew, Kirk had lived all his life with this old couple, but even I, who had no biological knowledge, knew that he did not belong to them. He was of different stock. He looked every man in the eye and touched his forelock to none. As I remember him he was tall for his age, straight as a mast, flat-backed, and uncommonly broad across the shoulders. His hair was red, and he wore it very long, except when Baggie put a bowl on top of it and cut round the rim, and then he was a sorry sight — but nobody ever laughed at him. At least, no boy did.

The most remarkable thing about him was his eyes. I never noticed the colour of anyone else's eyes until I grew up and started looking at girls, but I could not help noticing Kirk's. They were greenish-blue, the colour of blue-bottle flies in the sun, and they were full of devil. When Kirk flicked me with these blue-bottle eyes of his and said, 'What are we waiting for?' I just automatically said, 'Let's go.' I always said it, and I always went. I guess I'd have gone anywhere at all with Kirk.

Kirk was a year and nine months older than me. When he was ten he built a boat out of three-ply wood and petrolcans, and we sailed this boat on the open sea. We were often afloat for the whole day, and sometimes we went so far out to sea that we lost sight of land. When it blew up we shipped a lot of water, and then I baled like fury with two Rowntree cocoa tins while Kirk sat cross-legged in the stern, keeping her bows up to the seas by judicious management of his oar (my sister's tennis racket with the gut out and a sheet of tin nailed in its place). He was never at a loss, never rattled — never afraid — and twenty years ago I had much the same degree of confidence in Kirk and his three-ply *Ruler of the Waves* as I now have in Captain Illingworth and the *Queen Mary*.

One day during an aquatic gala in the harbour of a small town-nine or ten miles up the coast, Kirk paddled through the bottle-neck into the basin, and allowed himself to be captured by the judges' launch. When they asked where he had come from, he pointed out to sea and said, 'Norge.' The local folks made a great fuss of him, presented him to Lady somebody or other who was there for the prize-giving, fed him on chocolate and ice-cream, and billeted him with the Minister. The Minister had then three young daughters — one of whom is now my wife — and she has told me that Kirk made such a powerful impression, what with slapping his chest, emitting guttural growls, and declaiming, 'Ach so?' that she and her sisters were all slightly in love with him for weeks.

The imposture lasted less than a day, but it happened to be the day the weekly county paper went to press, and our normally reliable journal came out with a sober account of Kirk's adventure under the heading, 'YOUNG VIKING'S EXPLOIT'.

In due course Kirk and his boat were sent home in one of Alexander's big blue buses, the story was the talk of the town, and my father, discovering that I had sometimes gone to sea with Kirk, thrashed me judicially and, with an axe over his shoulder, marched me down to Baggie's cottage, where he fulminated against Kirk and duly dispatched the boat. It is characteristic of Kirk that while my father was telling Baggie exactly what he meant to do to *that boy* if ever he laid hands on him, that boy was grinning smugly down at us from a branch not six feet above my father's head.

Kirk was always one jump ahead of the other fellow. I am sure that was the secret of his leadership. When a gang of us went guddling, Kirk would coax a whole frying of sizeable trout into his thick fingers while the rest of us puddled with a few miserable sticklebacks. If we went along the cliffs to rob gulls' nests, it was Kirk who spotted the best colonies and only Kirk who would dare climb to them. It was Kirk who first showed us a bowline on the bight and a Turk's head, who made fish-hooks for us out of horse-shoe nails, who taught us to lift and cope a ferret, who assembled the radio for our KU-KLUX clubroom. He was a born leader. He was always out in front, and whenever there was anything important to be done it was always Kirk who did it best.

The people of my home town still talk about Kirk's jumping. The first time he jumped from the Brig o' Doom was one Sunday afternoon when he would have been about twelve. We had gone for a walk, the pair of us, and we were leaning over the parapet of the Brig looking for salmon swirls in the pool some sixty feet below when Kirk said, 'Bet you couldn't jump it.' I said, 'Bet you couldn't either,' and Kirk jumped it.

When I told them at school they wouldn't believe me, and I laid bets wholesale, and the following Saturday the whole school turned up to see Kirk jump from the Brig again. Everybody was scared stiff when he climbed up on the parapet, but after it was all over some of the older boys said it was easy enough that side, they'd like to see him do it on the other side, between the rocks, *that's* where they had bet he wouldn't jump. So Kirk jumped on the other side, between the rocks, and while he was jumping Alan Maxwell fainted, and at least half of us didn't dare look. Kirk said it was easy, he would jump it any time we wanted, but none of us who had seen him do it wanted to see him do it again. Of course there were some who had missed the fun, and so for several Saturdays Kirk, accompanied by bands of boys, went out to Doom, and for a collection of pennies, marbles, chewing-gum, etc., jumped from the Brig.

Next it was the Town Bridge. I don't know who first threw out the challenge by saying it was impossible to jump from the Town Bridge, it might have been any of us, for – goodness knows – we all knew very well how impossible it was. The Town Bridge is even higher than Doom, and there isn't more than five or six feet of water at the deepest point.

Kirk was to jump at ten o'clock on a Saturday morning, and by nine o'clock there was such a press of boys on the bridge that traffic was at a standstill, there were hooting lines of cars at both ends, and the police were out in force trying to move us on. When Kirk appeared, Sergeant Munro, I think it was, collared him and led him by the scruff of the neck to the police station. Kirk said he had a bad time in the police station, he didn't exactly get the third degree, but he had a thoroughly bad time; he was told all about Borstal, and he was told that he would be sent there, broken neck and all, if he ever dared jump from the Town Bridge. They kept him in the police station for over an hour, and when Kirk came out he said he would be there still if he hadn't finally promised, Scout's honour, that he wouldn't jump from the bridge.

Well, Kirk didn't jump.

He dived, and he got off lightly, breaking only his left arm and collar-bone and cracking open his skull across his two crowns.

He wasn't sent to Borstal, but he spent five weeks on his back in Palmer's Hospital.

When Kirk was thirteen Baggie said it was time he stopped scrimshanking and learned a trade. Actually Kirk had worked at odd jobs from the time he was able to walk – lifting potatoes, picking rasps, delivering papers and groceries, shovelling coke in the gasworks, helping mysteriously in the blacksmith's shop, and so on – but of course there wasn't any future in these jobs, and I suppose that Baggie was thinking only of what was best for Kirk when he decided to apprentice him to Old John Low, the tailor.

Kirk felt terrible about it. He said flatly that he wasn't going to be a tailor. He wasn't going to do woman's work in a stuffy shop, not him, he had set his heart on the sea, and he was going to sea and be damned to them all. There were some desperate scenes in the cottage at the foot of the hill, and after one of them, when Baggie had thrashed him with a strap, Kirk ran away. He was caught in Aberdeen on board an Icelandic trawler and sent home, and he spent exactly one day at work in the tailor's shop. On the evening of that day Baggie came up to our house and, with a great flurry of lock-touching, asked to see my father.

'It's aboot ma loon, Kirk,' he said, panting.

'Fit's wrang wi' your loon?' our maid asked.

'Ma loon's took the chopper and chopped off his thimble finger,' Baggie said.

My father listened in amazement to the story and gave his advice. His advice was to send the boy to sea, and the sooner the better.

Kirk was duly sent to sea and disappeared from my life. I wrote him twice, addressing my letters to the Assistant Cook aboard the trawler *Esmeralda*, c/o the Aberdeen Trawling Company, but I did not get any reply. I have not seen Kirk since that day nearly twenty years ago when he came to say good-bye with all his worldly possessions in a small sack on his back and his right hand still in bandages.

But although I have not seen him I have thought of him often. At moments of crisis my mind seems always to have returned to Kirk, and I am deeply conscious of having hitched my wagon to the stars which he, in childhood, showed me. It was Kirk who taught me by his example that a man must be true to himself, no matter what the cost, and that lesson has stood me in good stead at all the crossroads in my life. It was because of Kirk's example that I dug my heels in and insisted that I was going to be a writer, not a doctor. It was because of Kirk that, when war broke out, I chose to go to sea rather than join Naval Intelligence and sit in an office job ashore. And then, during the war, when things happened to me – when my ship was blown up under me in the North Sea, when I was attacked by a pack of U-boats on Atlantic convoy, and when I swept five mines in twenty minutes off Normandy on D-day minus one – it was mainly because I had moulded my life on Kirk that I was able to behave, in these testing moments, in a way that I like to think was adequate. Again and again I have found myself thinking of that red-headed boy, imagining him as a much-decorated fighter pilot, as a parachutist on a hopeless mission, as the leader of a suicidal guerrilla band, and whenever I have felt my spirits flag, when I have been faced with a problem that has seemed too big for me, I have summoned up a picture of Kirk and I have asked myself, 'What would *he* do?' And of course the thing that Kirk would do has always been the thing which has been most difficult for me to do, but it has also been the right thing – and once in a while I've done it.

I owe Kirk a debt that I can never repay.

Although I have not seen him since we were boys together, I *have* heard of him. On Christmas Eve, 1945, when we were clearing the last of the Mediterranean minefields, a Sammy mine popped up underneath my ship and blew her stern off. We were towed into Algiers, and those officers who had lost their gear went ashore to find a tailor.

They found a very good one in a little shop off the *place du Gouvernement,* a genial and characterful Scotsman who had lost a finger fighting pirates in the China Seas. They were pleased with the gear he sold them, and they brought back his card and stuck it on the wardroom notice-board. Translated, it read:

KIRK McLAUGHLIN
European Tailor
75 rue Bab Azoun, Algiers
CLASSY CLOTHES FOR CLASSY GENTS

It was unmistakably Kirk.

Sunday Class

ELSPETH DAVIE

This semicircle crouched around the teacher are dead on time with their answers. A well-drilled lot, they flick them back, one after the other, while the question is scarcely out of her mouth.

'Flowers.'

'Birds.'

'Good food.'

'Homes.'

'Friends.'

'And loved ones,' snaps the oldest girl jealously.

Now they all turn their heads to the boy at the end. They know there is nothing left for him except 'good books', 'good music' or perhaps 'sunshine' at a pinch. They wait for it. He stares stubbornly down towards the end of the room.

'Come on,' urges the woman, Miss MacRae, her eyes wavering from her lapel brooch to her wrist-watch. 'Some of the things God wants us to be grateful for?'

'Dinosaurs,' says the boy.

There is a pause while the woman shifts the fur about her neck. She looks warm. 'To be *grateful* for,' she warns.

'I know that. I said "dinosaurs".'

'I suppose you know what they are?'

'I know all about them. Always have.'

'And you know how to spell them?'

'It doesn't matter.'

'What did you say?'

'It doesn't matter.'

'Can you not think of anything else?'

'No. I'm thinking of them all the time.'

'*All* the time?' Her eyes narrow in suspicion.

'Well, someone had better think about them. They were around for millions of years. I'm grateful for them!'

There is reason to be grateful for the swinge and whack of the monstrous, scaly tails in this stifling hall. A quiver of relief runs through the others in the circle as they momentarily throw aside good books, homes and loved ones. They stare up towards the high sealed windows expectantly. In this East of Scotland town it is common enough to see things swirling in the air even at that height. On the stormiest days tufts of foam have sailed past and whole sodden newspapers flattened themselves out against the glass. Besides being a meeting-place for various classes during the week this hall is sometimes used for a dance, and on Sunday morning the sweaty dust of Saturday night still hangs in the air. On the platform stands a grand piano, swathed in green cloth. Along the wall behind it are various Bible pictures, maps and travel posters. There is also a chart showing a fair-haired young man balancing on the apex of a large iso-sceles triangle, and at graded levels beneath him a variety of animals stare wonderingly up, except for one or two leathery creatures near the bottom who continue to stare glumly at their own tails. The chap standing at the top looks glad to be where he is, but not surprised. He is not naked, as in some charts, but wears a casual sports shirt and flannel trousers. His pink, open palms are turned outwards to show that he has nothing to hide. His bare feet are also turned outwards.

Down both sides of the room, separated from one another by thin, wooden screens, are a dozen or so small circles seated around a man or a woman. From behind each screen comes a strange murmuring, discreet and low. It is like the murmurings of visitors in a hospital ward – sometimes placating, sometimes insistent or impatient, but always mesmerically soft. The boy who has dinosaurs on the brain keeps turning his head first to the stage and then to the door. Sometimes he tips his chair forward and cranes his neck as though to see around the neighbouring screens and to catch another murmur, perhaps to compare one murmur with another. Then he returns his attention to the woman in front of him, watching her mouth closely like a lip-reader or like somebody following a conversation in a foreign language. This irritates her more than anything else.

'I'm afraid that's not quite good enough,' she insists. 'I want something more.'

The rest of the class fix him with their eyes. They are afraid that now for the sake of peace he will hand her a good book or even a single perfect flower. But the boy broods. Now he is dredging through the deepest pits of the sea. Things not quite good enough for Miss MacRae spurt from fissures or prod the blackness with phosphorescent eye-stalks. Further up are creatures frilled, beaked and scalloped, some whip-thin, others round and smooth as bells. And far above in steaming tropical forests the ground crackles and glitters with ferocious insects. He has made his choice. He scratches his knee thoughtfully, then raises his hands and demonstrates something in the air.

'There's a sort of insect —' he ruminates. 'A giant fish-killing bug with claws that fold up under its head like a clasp-knife . . .'

'I am taking no notice of you,' Miss MacRae interrupts instantly, her eyes riveted on him. 'Everybody else can understand what I'm asking. Are you different from everyone else?' He is silent. They are all silent, studying Miss MacRae. In striking contrast to her lack of love for wildlife she is made up of scraps from various birds and beasts. She is sporting a tuft of bright-coloured feathers, a couple of paws, a tail and a head and a carved bone or two. Her gloves are suede and she has a small purse-bag made of real pigskin lined with coarse hair. There is nothing artificial about her except the butterfly brooch in her lapel and the deep-set button eyes in the furry head that peers over her shoulder.

At the top of the room a handbell is struck loudly — signal that it is time to reassemble in the larger adjoining hall. Although most of the group snatch up magazines and bibles and stampede off as usual, a few — mostly the older girls — linger as though protectively about Miss MacRae. Today there are mixed feelings about her. Her dismissal of dinosaurs and her withdrawal from fish-killing bugs has shown her to be wildly outside and utterly alone. It seems there is no place to put her now. All the same some of them feel for her in their hearts, and the oldest girl strokes the face of the little fox consolingly.

But the boy remains uncompromisingly stern. He gives them all time to clear off to the next room and in the meantime he takes a closer look at the chart on the wall behind the platform. This look confirms something he has suspected for a long time. Now there is no doubt about it. Miss MacRae is the true, self-appointed mate of the chap standing on the sharp, topmost point of the isosceles triangle. Her place is up there beside him. But could the man bring himself to step aside one fraction of an inch to make room for her?

The Mystery of the Beehive

BERNARD MAC LAVERTY

The boy stood on the deck waving to his mother as the boat pulled out. He waved until she became a small figure with an upturned, white face. The dockside buildings began to get smaller and smaller and gave Brendan a strange feeling of loneliness. It was the first time he had ever been away from home by himself. He thrust his hands deep into his anorak pockets and spat over the side. When it hit the wind the spit turned at a sharp right-angle.

At school they had been reading about the potato famine and he imagined himself as one of the exiles, one of the people who had had to leave or else starve to death. The teacher had said that an exile was somebody who had to leave his native country when he didn't want to. Brendan felt like that now.

He was going on holiday to Scotland to his uncle's farm – a man he had only met once before in his life. There would be nobody to play with because his uncle and aunt had no children. But his mother had insisted that he should get away from the streets of Belfast for at least part of the summer.

The wind blew his hair and he felt cold enough to shiver. He went into the lounge, found a seat and ate the sandwiches his mother had made for him. He wondered what the farm would be like. With a small start of panic he wondered what would

92

happen if his uncle didn't recognize him when he got to the other side.

But he needn't have worried. His Uncle Michael was there at the quayside, waving and smiling. When they met they shook hands awkwardly. His uncle's hand was huge and as rough as sandpaper.

There was a smell of pigs in the car as they drove northwards through the town and out into the country where yellow broom, the colour of butter, grew all along the side of the road. Brendan sat forward so that he could see his uncle's face better. He hadn't shaved and his chin was all bristly with copper-coloured hairs. His cap was pulled down almost to his nose so that to see to drive he had to tilt his head back. Uncle Michael talked in a loud voice asking him how his parents were and how they were standing up to the troubles in Belfast. He asked Brendan if his Da had grown any hair on his baldy head.

Brendan laughed, 'Have you got any hair, Uncle Michael?'

'I have, but it's all round the edges,' he said and lifted his cap to show his bald dome sticking up through the red hair.

As they drove along, the smell of pigs became so awful that Brendan asked if he could open a window. No sooner had he opened it than the car was filled with a buzzing noise. Brendan cowered back as the insect dashed itself from one window to another.

'It's only a bee,' said his uncle, looking round at him. But when he saw how frightened the boy was he stopped the car and shooed it out with his hand.

'I'm not afraid of bees,' said Brendan, but his voice was shaking and he looked a bit pale.

'You don't have to be tough with me,' said his uncle. 'It takes a brave man to be afraid. You'll have to get used to them because there are bees on the farm.'

When they arrived, Brendan was a bit disappointed. He didn't know what he had expected but it wasn't this. A scatter of red-leaded outbuildings, a paved yard, the house itself. It was old – a bungalow type with attic rooms sticking out of the roof. His Aunt Betty met him at the door with a big smile, wiping her hands on her apron.

'Come in,' she said. 'You must be starving.'

As they sat down to the neatly-laid table Uncle Michael laughed and said, 'Somebody important must be coming. We've got the tablecloth on.'

Without saying a word Aunt Betty took his cap off and set it on the radio then hit him a tiny clap on his bald head. 'Get on with your tea,' she said.

Brendan was just trying to answer Aunt Betty's questions and eat at the same time when he heard a heavy thumping step in the hallway. The door opened and Brendan stared, his eyes widening. A masked figure stood on the threshold. The figure was dressed in white — wide-brimmed white hat, white smock, white gloves and a white nylon mask covering his face.

When Uncle Michael saw Brendan's face he laughed and said, 'There's no need to worry — you're not in Belfast now. This is Mr Zveginzov. He's our beekeeper.'

Brendan laughed, feeling a bit ashamed. Mr Zveginzov took off his gloves, then his hat with the covering muslin. He was very old and slightly stooped. He had a blunt face and his hair was white and stubble-cut. His mouth was pulled down sourly at the corners. The eyelid of his left eye drooped, like a half-drawn window blind. He nodded brusquely to the new guest, then stomped heavily up the stairs to his room. In his hand Brendan noticed a small canvas bag.

'You mustn't worry about Zveginzov,' said Aunt Betty. 'He's a little bit odd, but he's very nice really. He has his routines, his little ways.'

'And you can't blame him,' said Uncle Michael, 'he's been through a lot.'

'Yes,' Aunt Betty nodded. 'He just called at the door one night. He wanted to work for something to eat. We took him in and he's been a sort of boarder ever since.'

Brendan asked about his funny name and Aunt Betty told him that Mr Zveginzov was a Jew who had lived in Russia a long time ago. He had left his country because of the pogroms.

'The what?' asked Brendan.

'Pogroms,' said his aunt. 'That's just another name for a sort of riot. Some Russian people hated the Jews and they stoned them and beat them. They drove them out of their homes and even killed them because they were Jewish.'

'I know,' said Brendan.

'So Zveginzov ran away from Russia and wandered the world until the night he ended up here. Be kind and polite to him and you should get on well together.'

After lunch Brendan went out to play and explore the farm. Beyond the paved yard were the open fields and the hills covered in patches of gorse, yellow on dark green. Higher on the hillside it gave way to purple heather. A small trout stream, brown and crystal and flecked with foam, splashed its crooked way down from the mountain.

On his way back to the house he discovered a long vegetable garden. At the bottom was a clear area with six beehives sitting on the grass. Brendan sat and watched from a safe distance the bees coming and going. The air was filled with their constant buzzing drone. He thought of the man's funny name and said it over and over again. He loved repeating words – even the simplest ones – until they lost their meaning.

'Zveginzov, Zveginzov, Zveginzov.' He thought it sounded like the bees. 'Zveginzov.' He pulled and chewed a stalk of grass. Already he was a bit bored.

He went back to the house just as his Aunt Betty was finishing the dishes. 'Which room am I sleeping in?' he asked.

Aunt Betty dried her hands on the roller towel on the back of the door and led him through the hallway. 'Your room is downstairs at the back of the house,' she said.

Brendan looked out through the small panes of the window. Outside was a beautiful tree. He couldn't remember seeing one like it ever. It was small and looked old and gnarled but its yellow beaded blossoms hung down like gold, like necklaces.

'What sort of tree is that?' he asked.

'Oh yes, I'm glad you reminded me. Good boy Brendan. You must never touch that tree because it's poisonous. It's a laburnum tree and if you ate one of those seeds – out of the little black pods – you would be dead before you could eat another one. With no children about the place you forget how dangerous it is. Promise me now you will not touch it.'

Brendan nodded and said over and over to himself 'laburnum, laburnum, laburnum' until it had no meaning.

'Another thing,' said Aunt Betty, pointing her finger at the ceiling, 'that is Mr Zveginzov's room straight above you so you must be as quiet as a mouse when he is in. All right?'

Brendan nodded and asked if he could go upstairs to explore but to his surprise his aunt answered sharply. 'No. You mustn't go upstairs and disturb Mr Zveginzov. This is his private time. He has asked us specially and we have agreed to it. That's another promise you'll have to keep.' Then she smiled at herself for having spoken so sharply. 'He's old,' she said, 'and not used to children.'

That night, as he lay in the strange bed with its faintly damp smell, Brendan couldn't sleep for hours. Outside the window the blossoms of the poisonous laburnum swung in the night breeze silently. He heard Mr Zveginzov come in and go up the creaking stairway. Above his head the heavy footsteps crossed and recrossed the floor for what seemed like most of the night. Brendan looked at the ceiling and saw the light-bulb tremble slightly at each step and wondered what was wrong with the old man.

The next day Brendan went to play on the haystacks in the field beside the vegetable garden. The sun came out and it was warm. The hay looked yellow and soft but when he tried to climb the haystack he found it hard and prickly. There was a small ladder against one stack and Brendan climbed this to slide down the other side. When he was on the top he could see over the hedge into the vegetable garden. He saw Mr Zveginzov come out of the house dressed in his beekeeper's clothes. Brendan slid down the haystack and crawled into the bottom of the hedge. He could see quite clearly Zveginzov walking empty-handed to the hives and when he opened one a black swarm of bees raced out and hovered around his head. They crawled on his hat and the nylon mask covering his face but he didn't seem to mind. Brendan shuddered at the thought of it — their furry bodies, their buzzing wings.

When Zveginzov came to the third hive he opened it with particular care. Brendan watched closely. Zveginzov crouched down and took out a small canvas bag. It was the same bag Brendan had seen him bring into the house the afternoon before. The old man stood up slowly and put his gloved hand to his back as if he was in pain. Then he walked through the vegetable garden back to the house carrying the canvas bag.

Brendan followed him back to the house and got in just in time to hear Zveginzov's footsteps going up the stairs to his room. Aunt Betty was baking some scones and he knew that he would be caught if he tried to sneak up after him. Besides he had made a promise that he wouldn't go up the stairs.

He went outside and sat in the garden looking up at Zveginzov's bedroom window. He hadn't pulled his curtains. The branches of the laburnum tree reached up and almost tapped the window pane. The hanging yellow flowers swayed in the light breeze. Brendan got up off the grass and went over to the tree. As he reached up his hand he thought of his aunt's warning. 'You mustn't even touch it.' He closed his hand round one of the flowers slowly and crushed it. He waited. He knew that touching a flower couldn't kill him.

It was an easy tree to climb, its branches old with plenty of grips for his hands and feet. As he climbed, the tree began to shake and all the hanging flowers trembled under his weight. He reached the branch level with Zveginzov's window. It was hard to see into the room because the sun had gone behind a cloud.

Gradually he made out Zveginzov's figure. He was slumped over the table with his face buried in his arms. On the table was the canvas bag – open but Brendan couldn't see into it. Then the old man moved. He ran his fingers through his short stubbly white hair and nodded his head from side to side. Then he dipped into the bag and took something out of it. He looked at it closer, but it was shielded from Brendan by his hand. Zveginzov looked down into the bag. The sun came out from behind the cloud, shining into the room, and Brendan saw a bright yellow reflected from the bag into the old man's face.

Zveginzov smiled, then suddenly he looked up and saw Brendan watching him from the tree. In a flash his look changed to one of anger and he jumped over to the window, his face white. Brendan leapt from the tree through a hiss of leaves and ran. He heard Zveginzov open the window and scream something after him but he didn't know what it was because it was in a different language.

All day Brendan sneaked about the house avoiding Mr Zveginzov and the next morning when he got up the old man had gone out. Aunt Betty set a plateful of her homemade scones on the breakfast table, then brought a section of honey to put on them. It was like a little wooden box, open at the top. Inside was a network of a white substance shaped like chicken wire.

'What's that?' asked Brendan.

'Beeswax,' said Aunt Betty. 'The bees make those little cells and then fill them with honey. You can eat that stuff. It's nice and crunchy.' Brendan dipped his knife into the honeycomb and spread some on his scone.

'Yes, the honey here is a good flavour because of the heather,' said Aunt Betty. 'And Mr Zveginzov looks after them well. It's like gold, isn't it? The colour I mean.'

'Where is Mr Zveginzov?' asked Brendan.

'I think he's gone to town. He goes to town every Friday,' she said, and left him to eat his breakfast. As he ate, Brendan thought about the canvas bag. What could be in it? Why did the old man hide it in the beehives? By the time he had finished his breakfast he had decided that there was only one way to find out.

He tiptoed into the hallway, lifted Zveginzov's beekeeping clothes that were hanging there and slipped into the vegetable garden. He put on the straw hat and made it fit by tying it tight with the mask. Then the smock, which hung down over his wrists. The gloves had elastic cuffs to stop the bees crawling up the sleeves but they were too loose on Brendan. Now he was scared and shaking a little. He had heard of people who died from bee-stings. As he came near the hives the sound of the bees grew louder and louder. One or two flew into the mask protecting his face and he brushed them away with his glove.

The sun was shining and he became very hot and uncomfortable under all the clothes. He felt sweat on his upper lip. He reached the third hive and rested his hand on it. Immediately thousands of bees, with what sounded like a roar, came streaming out of the hive and encircled his head. He clenched his teeth. So many bees had come out that he thought the hive must be empty but when he opened it thousands more poured out, their furry black and yellow bodies bumping into his veil, crawling over his chest and shoulders.

He looked into the hive past the swirling bees but could see no canvas bag. It was in the next hive that he found it. Immediately he turned and ran with it to the house end of the garden. When he was sure that no bees had followed him he took off the hat and mask. The gloves made his hand too clumsy to open the bag so he had to pull them off. It was closed with a draw-string at the neck. His excited fingers fumbled with the cord.

Brendan was so interested in the canvas bag that he didn't notice a movement behind him. Then a twig snapped under the weight of someone's foot. Brendan looked up. Zveginzov stood over him. His lips were drawn back in anger and his eyelid half dropped — like the blind in a house where someone had just died. He snatched the bag from Brendan.

'You nosey brat!' he shouted. Brendan thought he was going to strike him with his upraised hand but instead he rubbed the short white hair of his head. Suddenly the old man's face crumpled up and he began to cry. Brendan stood watching him, not knowing what to do. The tears ran down Zveginzov's face. He squatted down on the ground and when he spoke the anger had gone out of his voice.

'If you want to know so much what's in the bag, I will show you.' He opened it and let the boy look in. A hoard of gold coins gleamed at the bottom. Zveginzov took one out. It had strange writing on it around an eagle with spread wings. He turned it over and on the other side was a man's head.

'That is the Tzar's head,' he said. 'What I hold is a gold rouble. The only thing that I take with me out of Russia.' The tears were still wet on his face. Brendan repeated to himself the word 'rouble, rouble, rouble' until it had no meaning.

'And here is something else,' said Zveginzov, taking a tiny bag out of the larger one. 'Do you know what is in that?'

Brendan opened it. There was some dirt at the bottom of it but nothing else.

'It is the soil of Russia.' Brendan looked at him, not understanding. 'Let me tell you then. You left your own country to come here, is that not so? Do you know how you would have been feeling if you had to leave it for ever?' Brendan nodded. 'How would you feel if you had nothing to make you remember? I took these roubles, I took this – how you say – handful of soil to remind me of my dear, dear Russia.' The tears came to his eyes again.

'But if you loved it so much why did you leave it?'

'You ask me why I leave,' said Zveginzov. 'When somebody they burn your house from over your head, when somebody they kill your mother, when everybody they stone and spit at you – you do not stay in that place. It is time to go. I was the age of you, maybe, when my Papa took me and my brother and we ran. He gave me this bag to carry because he knew the soldiers would stop him with his black beard and his face of a Jew. And they did. The soldiers they killed my brother and Papa. Me they did not kill because I hid in a cellar. You ask me why I leave? You see this eye. I tell you how my eye happened. My brother and my Papa lie dead on the street. There is dust in his beard and my brother's eyes they are open. There is a little sign around my Papa's neck telling the world he is a Jew. I go to them to say goodbye and I kneel in the dust of the street. And what happens? A boy of my own age – of your age – sees me and lifts a stone, as sharp as a knife, and he throws it in my eye. Then he spits for hate of me. I run and I do not know where I am running because my eye is as full of blood as his heart is full of hate. And you ask me why I leave?'

Brendan looked at his drooping eyelid and the blank staring eye behind it. He asked, 'But why did you keep your gold in the beehive?'

'Memories you cannot keep in a bank. I want to see my roubles. Each day I want to touch my soil. Where is gold safer than in a beehive?' The old man shrugged his shoulders and put his hands on his head. Brendan cleared his throat and said that he was sorry.

Zveginzov smiled, 'To be young is to be nosey,' he said. 'But you must keep my secret.' Zveginzov dipped two fingers into the bag and produced a gold coin which he gave to Brendan. He made him promise never to spend it but to keep it all his life to remember an old man who had lost his country.

Silver Linings

JOAN LINGARD

Every cloud is supposed to have one, or so I learned at my granny's knee. Isn't that where you're supposed to learn such things? My granny is full of sayings, most of them rubbish, according to my mother, who has her own sayings. Like most mothers. My granny isn't one of those grandmothers who sits and knits in the chimney corner, shrouded in shawls, if such grannies exist at all. She tints her hair auburn and is employed as manageress at a local supermarket. It's not all that 'super', I must add, as it's only got two aisles, one up and one down, but still, a job's a job these days. And money doesn't grow . . .

Money's a problem in our family and my granny helps keep us afloat with 'care' parcels. She dumps them down on the kitchen table muttering about the improvidence of my parents and the wasted education of my mother who had all the chances in life that she didn't have herself. Etcetera. My father is not a lot of use when it comes to providing. He does odd jobs and he comes and goes. Like driftwood, says my granny, who doesn't understand what her daughter saw in him.

I think it was probably his name. He's called Torquil. My mother's got a thing about names. Her own given name was Isobel. A good plain no-nonsense Scottish Christian name. The only person who uses it now is my granny. My mother is known to everyone else as Isabella or Bella.

My name is Samantha, which my mother uses in full, but my friends call me Sam and my brother's called Seb, short for Sebastian. My granny approves of neither the short nor the long versions. 'Sam and Seb — sounds like two cartoon characters!' She hates having to introduce us, it gives her a 'red face'. She had wanted us to be called Jean and Colin. So she calls me hen and Seb, son.

Anyway, to get back to silver linings. I don't know about clouds having them but for a short time we had in our possession a fur coat which had one. But, first, I'd better explain about my mother's shop.

She keeps a second-hand clothes shop in a street that's full of shops selling second-hand things, from books to old fenders and clocks to medals and feather boas (though they're scarce) and silk petticoats (usually full of snaps and runs) and woollens (usually washed in). There are also two or three bars in the street, and some cafés. We like it, Seb and I. There's always something going on. The shop's in a basement (a damp one) across the road from our flat. You can doubtless imagine what my granny thinks of it. She says the smell of the old clothes turns her stomach and folk that buy stuff like that need their heads examined.

But people do come in and buy, not that it's ever like the shops in Princes Street on a Saturday. And they tend to sit on boxes and blether to my mother for hours before they get round to buying some ghastly looking dress with a V neck and a drooping hemline that was fashionable during the war. And then they find they haven't got quite enough money to pay for it so my mother says she'll get it from them the next time they're in. You can see why we need the care parcels.

When my mother goes out on the rummage for new stock — new old stock, that is — she just shuts up the shop and leaves a note on the door saying 'Back in ten minutes' or, if I'm home from school, she leaves me in charge with my friend Morag. (Nice name, Morag, says my granny.) Morag and I amuse ourselves by trying on the clothes and parading up and down

like models. We usually have a good laugh too. I like long
traily dresses in black crêpe de chine and big floppy hats and
Morag likes silks and satins. We don't bother with the washed-
in woollies.

One day my mother came back in a taxi filled to bursting
with old clothes. She was bursting with excitement too, even
gave the taxi driver a pound tip. You'd have thought we were
about to make our fortune!

Morag and I helped to haul in the catch. We sat on the floor
in the middle of it and unpacked the bags. There were dresses
of every colour of the rainbow, made of silk and of satin, of
brocade and of very fine wool.

'They belonged to an old lady,' said my mother.

The dresses smelt really old when you pressed them to your
face.

'She died last month.'

We shivered a little and let the dresses fall into our laps.

'She was *very* old though.'

We cheered up and turned our attention to the blouses and
scarves and the satin shoes. The old lady must never have
thrown anything away.

And then out of a bag I took a fur coat. Now my mother
doesn't like fur coats, usually won't handle them. By that, I
mean sell them. She's for Beauty Without Cruelty. As I am
myself. But this coat felt kind of smooth and silky, even though
it was a bit bald looking here and there, and so I slipped it on.

'I'll have to get rid of that quickly,' said my mother.

I stroked the fur.

'Poor animal,' said my mother.

I slipped my hands into the pockets. I was beginning to think
there was something funny about the coat. The lining felt odd,
sort of lumpy, and I thought I could hear a faint rustling noise
coming from inside it. I took the coat off.

The lining had been mended in a number of places by
someone who could sew very fine stitches. I lifted the scissors
and quickly began to snip the thread.

'What are you doing that for?' asked my mother irritably.

'Wait!'

I eased my hand up between the lining and the inside of the coat and brought out a five pound note. Morag gasped. And then I brought out another and another and then a ten pound one and then another five and a ten —

'I don't believe it!' said my mother, who looked as pale as the off-white blouse she was crumpling between her hands.

We extracted from the lining of the coat one thousand and ten pounds in old bank notes. They were creased and aged, but they were real enough. We sat in silence and stared at them. My mother picked up a ten pound note and peered at it in the waning afternoon light.

'She can't have trusted the bank. Old people are sometimes funny that way. Keep their money in mattresses and places.' Like old coats.

'We could go for a holiday,' I said.

'A Greek island,' murmured my mother. 'Paros. Or Naxos.'

Once upon a time she used to wander around islands, with my father, before Seb and I were born. I could see us, the three of us, lying on the warm sand listening to the soft swish of the blue blue sea.

'Are you going to keep it?' asked Morag, breaking into our trance. She's a bit like that, Morag, down-to-earth, a state of being that my granny is fully in favour of.

My mother bit the side of her lip, the way she does when she's a bit confused. She quite often bites her lip.

'Finder's keepers,' I said hopefully. Hadn't my granny taught me that?

'I did *pay* for the coat.'

Not a thousand pounds of course, we knew that.

'Who did you buy it from?' asked Morag.

'A relative of the old lady's. He was clearing out the house. He looked well enough heeled.'

'In that case —' I said.

'I'll need to think about it,' said my mother. 'In the meantime —' She glanced about her and I got up to put on the light and draw the curtains.

What *were* we to do with the money?

'We could sew it back into the coat,' I suggested.

That seemed as good an idea as any other so Morag and I pushed the notes back into the lining, all but one ten pound one which my mother said we might as well keep out to buy something for supper with that evening.

'Morag,' she said, sounding a bit awkward, 'don't be saying anything about this to anyone else eh?'

'I wouldn't dream of it, Isabella.' (My mother likes my friends to call her by her Christian name. She likes Seb and me to do it too but when I'm talking about her I always refer to her as 'my mother'.)

When I chummed Morag along the street on her way home I told her I'd kill her if she did tell and we almost quarrelled as she said I'd no business to doubt her word. But it was such a big secret to keep! I felt choked up with the excitement of it.

We took the fur coat across the road with us when we went home and over an Indian carry-out and a bottle of rosé wine my mother and Seb and I discussed the problem of whether we were entitled to keep the money or not. Seb and I thought there was no problem at all.

'You bought the coat, Bella,' said Seb. 'Everything in it's yours.'

'Well, I don't know. Maybe legally, but morally . . . I mean, I suppose I *should* give it back.'

'But you want to go to Greece don't you?' I said.

Her lip trembled.

Outside, it was raining. Big heavy drops were striking the window pane and the wind was making the glass rattle in its frame.

'You could both be doing with new shoes,' said our mother. 'Mind you, with money like that . . .' She sighed.

The next day was Saturday. We took the coat back over to the shop with us in the morning, afraid to let it out of our sight. My mother put it in a cupboard in the back room where she keeps garments that are waiting to be mended. Some are beyond redemption but they wait nevertheless.

In the afternoon, we had to go to a family wedding, on my father's side. My father was supposed to be there. My mother and I kitted ourselves out with clothes from the shop.

'Well, honestly!' declared my granny, on her arrival. She was to mind the shop while we were gone. 'I could have lent you a nice wee suit, Isobel.' She turned to look me over. 'Do you think black crêpe de chine's the right thing to be wearing at a wedding? And at your age too!' She didn't even call me hen. She couldn't have thought I looked endearing. The dress had come out of the old lady's wardrobe.

In the bus, Seb said to our mother, 'Now don't tell Father about the money if he *is* there.'

He did turn up. He was his usual 'charming' self, never stuck for words. I was pleased enough to see him to begin with but after a bit when I saw him sweet-talking our mother and her cheeks beginning to turn pink and her eyes lighting up, I felt myself going off him. Seb and I sat side by side and drank as much fizzy wine as we could get hold of and listened to her laugh floating down the room.

'She'll tell him,' said Seb gloomily.

She did of course. And he decided to come home with us. They walked in front of us holding hands.

'When will she ever learn?' said Seb, sounding strangely like our granny.

'Good evening, Torquil,' said that lady very stiffly, when we came into the shop where she was sitting playing Clock Patience on the counter top. 'Stranger,' she couldn't resist adding.

'Hi, Ma!' He gave her a smacking kiss on the cheek. 'It's good to see you. You're not looking a day older.'

She did not return the compliment.

'Been busy?' asked my mother.

'Not exactly rushed off my feet. I sold two or three dresses and one of those tatty Victorian nightgowns – oh, and yon moth-eaten fur coat in the cupboard through the back.'

She might just as well have struck us all down with a sledge-hammer. We were in a state of total collapse for at least five minutes until my mother managed to get back the use of her tongue.

'You sold *that coat*?'

'Well, why not? You hate having fur lying around.'

'Who did you sell it to?' My mother was doing her best to stay calm.

'How should I know? Some woman. She came in asking if we'd any furs. She gave me twenty pounds for it. I didn't think you could ask a penny more. Lucky to get that.'

My mother told my granny about the money in the lining and then it was her turn to collapse. I thought we were going to have to call a doctor to revive her. My father managed it with some brandy that he had in his coat pocket.

'Oh no,' she moaned, 'oh *no*. But what did you leave it in the shop for, Isobel?'

'It was in the back shop! In the cupboard.'

They started to argue, to blame one another. Seb and I went out and roamed the streets till dark and long after looking for the woman in our fur coat. We never did see it again.

Our father left the next morning.

'Shows him up for what he is, doesn't it?' said our granny. 'He only came back for the money. He'd have taken you to the cleaners, Isobel. Maybe it was just as well. As I always say —' She stopped.

Not even she had the nerve to look my mother in the eye and say that every cloud has its silver lining.

The Blot

IAIN CRICHTON SMITH

Miss Maclean said, 'And pray tell me how did you get the blot on your book?'

I stood up in my seat automatically and said, 'It was ... I put too much ink in the pen, please, miss.' I added again forlornly, 'Please, miss.' She considered or seemed to consider this for a long time, but perhaps she wasn't really thinking about it at all, perhaps she was thinking about something else. Then she said, 'And did you not perhaps think of putting less ink in your pen? I imagine one has a choice in those matters.' The rest of the class laughed as they always did, promptly and decorously, whenever Miss Maclean made a joke. She said, 'Be quiet', and they stopped laughing as if one of the taps mentioned in our sums had been switched off. Miss Maclean always wore a grey thin blouse and a thin black jacket. Sometimes she seemed to me to look like a pencil.

'Do you not perhaps believe in having a tidy book as the rest of us do?' she said. I didn't know what to say. Naturally I believed in having a tidy book. I liked the whiteness of a book more than anything else in the world. To write on a white page was like ... how can I say it? ... it was like a bird leaving footprints in snow. But then to say that to her was to sound daft. And anyway, why couldn't she clean the globe which lay in front of her on the desk? It was always dusty so that you could leave your fingerprints all over Europe or South America or Antigua. Antigua was a really beautiful name; I had come across it recently in an atlas. The highest mark she ever gave for an essay was five out of ten, and she was always spoiling jotters by filling them with comments and scoring through words and adding punctuation marks. But I must admit that when she wrote on the board she wrote very neatly.

'And what's this,' she said, 'about an old woman? I thought you were supposed to write about a postman. Have you never seen a postman?' She was always asking stupid questions like that. Of course I had seen a postman. 'And what's this word "solatary"? I presume you mean "solitary". You shouldn't use big words unless you can spell them. And whoever saw an old woman peering out through the letter-box when the postman came up the stairs? You really have the oddest notions.' The class laughed again. No, I had not actually seen an old woman peering through a letter-box, but there was no reason why one shouldn't, why my old woman shouldn't. In fact she *had* been peering through the letter-box. I was angry at having misspelt 'solitary'. I didn't know how I had come to do that, since I knew the correct spelling. 'Old women don't look through letter-boxes waiting for letters,' she almost screamed, her face reddening with rage.

Why did she hate me so much? I wondered. It was the same when I wrote the essay about the tiger who ate fish and chips. Was it really because my work wasn't neat and because I was always putting ink-blots on the paper? My hands were clumsy, there was no getting away from that. They never did what I wanted them to do. Her hands, however, were very thin and neat, ringless. Not like my mother's hands. My mother's hands were wrinkled and one of the fingers had a plain gold ring which she could never get off.

'Old women don't spend their time waiting for letters,' she shouted. 'They have other things to do with their time. I have never seen an old woman who waited every day for a letter. Have you? HAVE you?'

I thought for some time and then said, 'No, miss.'

'Well then,' she said, breathing less heavily. 'But you always want to be clever, don't you? I asked you to write about a postman and you write about an old woman. That is impertinence. ISN'T IT?'

I knew what I was expected to answer so I said, 'Yes, miss.'

She looked down at the page from an enormous height with her thin hawk-like gaze and read out a sentence in a scornful voice. ' "She began to write a letter to herself but as she did so a blot of ink fell on the page and she stopped." Why did you write that? That again is deliberate insolence.'

'It came into my mind at that . . . after I had put the ink on my jotter. It just came into my head.'

'It was insolence, wasn't it? WASN'T IT?'

Actually it hadn't been. It had been a kind of inspiration. The idea came into my head very quickly and I had written the sentence before I thought how it would appear to her. I hadn't been thinking of her when I was writing the composition. But from now on I would have to think of her, I realized. Whatever I wrote I would have to think of her reading it and the thought filled me with despair. I couldn't understand why her face quivered with rage when she spoke to me, why she showed such hatred. I didn't want to be hated. Who wanted to be hated like this?

I felt this even while she was belting me. Perhaps she was right. Perhaps it had been insolence. Perhaps neatness was the most important thing in the world. After she had belted me she might be kind to me again and she might stop watching me all the time as if I was an enemy. The thing was, I must learn to hide from her, be neat and clean. Maybe that would work, and her shouting would go away. But even as I thought that and was writhing with pain from the belt, I was also thinking, Miss Maclean, very clean, Miss Maclean, very clean. The words shone without my bidding in front of my head. I was always doing that. Sums, numbs, bums, mums. I also thought, Have you Macleaned your belt today? I thought of a story where a dirty old man, a tramp sitting by the side of the road, would shout, 'Why aren't you as clean as me?' The tramp was very like old Mackay who worked on the roads and was always singing hymns, while breaking the rock. And there was another story where the belt would stand up like a snake and sway to music. In front of her thin grey blouse the belt would rise, with a snake's head and a green skin. I could even hear the accompanying music, staccato and vibrant. It was South American music and came from the dusty globe in front of her.

Touch and Go!

DAVID TOULMIN

It was a dark winter's night that Wee Tam's mither and Mrs
Lunan, a neighbour body, planned a raid on a nearby farmer's
henhouse. Mrs Lunan's man was a cripple, and they lived in an
old croft house down in the howe of Glenshinty. They had
three or four bairns running barefoot around the place, with
hardly a stitch of clothing on their backs, but somehow they
managed to scrape along on a mere pittance from the Assistance
Board, and once in a while the Inspector of the Poor looked in
by to see if the creatures were still alive.

'Ma man's been real poorly lately,' said Mrs Lunan, warming
her hands at the fire, 'and a drappie o' chicken bree wad do him
a world o' good.'

'But whaur are we gaun tae get a hen at this time o' nicht?'

'Steal ane,' said Mrs Lunan, unabashed.

'Steal ane!' cried Tam's mither, and she looked at the woman
half in sympathy, half in fear, wondering what she was going
to say next.

'Aye, we'll try auld Grimshaw's place; it's fine near the road
and naebody wad jalouse us there. Get on yer coat wife and gie
us a hand.'

'A' richt wifie, but it's a bit risky,' said Tam's mither, but-
toning up her coat; 'and Tam, put on yer bonnet and come

and watch the coast is clear for us, and see there's nae ferlies aboot.'

Wee Tam shut his book and shuddered. He had been reading *Robinson Crusoe*, a big book that he had got from the dominie, one of those old-fashioned editions with beautifully stencilled capitals at the beginning of each chapter, and with a short summary of the events therein related. The loon was just getting fully absorbed in this pirate and cutlass masterpiece when the women hatched their plan.

The lamp was lit and the blinds were down and Tam's father snored in the box-bed. He was an early bedder and missed much of the goings on in the hoose, but Tam felt that the old man had one eye open half the time and that he listened between the snores. But he never interfered, mither was boss. Flora, Tam's little sister, lay snugly at her father's back, curled like a buckie, a doll in her oxter, and Tam felt it was a pity he hadn't gone to bed, then perhaps the women wouldn't have bothered him.

It was inky black and bitter cold outside. A mass of stars spangled the sky, and Tam could pick out the Seven Sisters twinkling above the dark smudge of pinewood on the Berry Hill. But apart from the sough and flap of the wind the world was as silent as a graveyard.

Tam shivered in his thin jacket as he trudged on behind the women, trying to identify the adventure with what he had been reading in *Robinson Crusoe*. About a mile along the road they came to Grimshaw's place, a big croft by the roadside, which Tam passed every day going to school. There was a lean-to poultry shed at the gable of the steading, close by the road, but in full view of the kitchen door.

The women first went past the farmhouse, to make sure there were no lights in the windows, walking on the grass to quieten the sound of their footsteps, then came back to where Tam waited at the henhouse.

Tam watched and listened but nobody stirred, nothing but the faint smell of the sharn midden and the scent of stale peat smoke that came to his nostrils on the wind. Everybody was asleep at this hour so the two women crept into the henhouse.

They groped for a couple of good plump birds on the roost and
wrung their necks before a cackle escaped them. There was
some flapping of wings and a flutter of feathers when they
came out, but never a squawk from the dead birds. They put
the hens in a sack, closed the henhouse door and made off,
Wee Tam behind them, still walking on the grass, all as silent as
doomsday.

Safely home Tam went back to Robinson Crusoe Island,
thinking no more about the affair, glad to be back to the fire
and the lamplight, snug in the satisfaction that he could read till
his eyes closed without further interruption, for it was just past
midnight.

The women set to plucking the hens in the kitchen, while the
birds were still warm, which makes it easier to do, and cleaning
them, getting them ready for the dinner, maybe with a plate of
broth first and the hen to follow, but Mrs Lunan said she would
roast hers because she wanted the 'bree' for her sick man.

Tam got a helping when he got home from school, running
all the way at the thought of it, his satchel unstrapped and
under his arm, to save the thump of it on his back. And it had
been a rare treat, especially the stuffing and the white flesh
around the breast-bone, which mither had laid aside for him,
and his old man had never asked where the hen came from.

In the evening, after supper, Tam was lighting a cigarette
over the lamp glass on the kitchen table, when the local bobby
laid his bicycle against the unblinded window. Tam quickly
snibbed the fag in the fire, just as the bobby walked in, never
waiting for an answer to his knock on the door.

'Aye lad,' says the bobby, as he peeled off his leather gloves.
'I fairly caught ye that time. I suppose ye ken that sixteen is the
age for smokin'.'

Tam squeezed himself into the corner behind the meal barrel,
his surest refuge in times of trouble. He remembered the hen in
the dresser and he felt terribly guilty and afraid. His father was
seated by the fireside. The policeman turned to him and said:
'Don't ye know it's illegal for the lad tae smoke afore he's
sixteen?'

Tam's father scratched his balding head, tired from his day's work in the byres. 'Oh aye,' says he, wearily, 'but the laddie gie's me a hand in the byre, and for that I dinna grudge 'im a bit blaw at a fag.'

But the bobby was indignant. 'It's not a question of whether you can afford it man, but you're breaking the law!' He turned to Tam's mither, who was placing a chair for him – 'Woman,' he said, 'do ye allow this to go on in the hoose: the rascal smokin' and him still at school?'

'Oh aye, but the man's boss in the hoose here,' she lied, thankful that the tiny wish-bone from the hen was in the oven, and not on the crook over the range as it might have been. When it became thoroughly brittle Tam would share it with his little sister: each would take a splint of it in the crook of a little finger, make a wish and pull, and whoever had the broken end when the bone snapped would lose the wish.

The constable sat down on a hard chair in the middle of the cement floor, crossed his legs and laid his 'cheese-cutter' cap on his knee. He was so near the hen now he could have smelled it. He only had to reach over to open the dresser door and there was the skeleton of it, on a plate.

He was much nearer Tam's height on the varnished chair and the loon breathed a little more freely behind the meal barrel. Nevertheless he was still a mighty giant in the shabby little kitchen, his red face polished with stern authority and his silver buttons twinkling in the lamplight. Tam focused his attention on the bobby's putteed leg, which he kept swinging up and down over his knee, as if he wished to show off the highly polished boot at the end of it, a boot that would give you a hefty kick in the buttocks if he got near enough.

'Have ye seen ony strange characters in the vicinity?' the bobby asked, looking first at Tam's mither, and then at his father. 'Auld Sandy Grimshaw has missed some hens out of his shed, and says that by the mess of feathers ootside the door, he feels sure they have been stolen.'

Tam's father suddenly recalled his splendid dinner but swallowed the thought. 'No,' he said, trying to look unconcerned, 'no, we hinna seen a crater, not a crater!'

Tam's mither poured out a glass of Dr Watson's Tonic Stout

for the bobby, and one for her husband. It was the only hop
beverage in the house and she excelled in the brewing of it,
though she sometimes made broom wine in the summer, with a
taste like whisky.

'Ye ken auld Grimshaw's place?' the bobby asked, taking the
glass in his fat, beringed fingers.

'Aye,' said Tam's mither, wiping her hands on her apron, 'I
ken the fairm: it's at the top o' the quarry brae, nae far frae the
shop.'

'Aye, ye ken wuman, I'm nae supposed tae drink in uniform,
but in this case we'll mak' an exception.'

'Ach man, that stuff will never touch ye!' And Tam's mither
busied herself wiping the table of what she had spilled, for the
bottles were brisk and the froth had hit the roof when she
removed the corks.

Tam's wee sister came forward with her biggest doll and laid
it on the bobby's knee. He bent the doll forward in his huge
hand and it 'Ba-a-a-ed' pitifully, as if it had a tummy ache. He
only had to ask little Flora what Dolly had for dinner and he
had the case wrapped up.

But the local flat-foot was no Sherlock Holmes, and he
believed only what he saw; like loons smoking while still in
short breeks, or a poor farm servant chauving home against the
wind without a rear-light on his bicycle.

Otherwise there wasn't a feather of evidence in sight. The
wing feathers were tied in a bundle in the cubby-hole under the
loft stair. Tam's mither would wash them and use them to
brush her oat-cakes before she put them in the girdle over the
fire. The downs were concealed in a sack; she would stuff them
into a pillow after they had been fumigated. The cats had eaten
all the offal on the midden. There wasn't a shred of evidence
left anywhere in sight.

The bobby licked his lips and set the empty glass on the
table. 'Thanks mistress,' he said, wiping his moustache, 'that
was capital!'

He got up and put on his peaked cap and gloves, glowering
down at wee Tam behind the meal barrel. 'Ye can coont yersel'
lucky lad,' he said, 'lucky that I'm nae takin' ye tae the lock-up.

Gin yer mither hadna been sic a gweed-he'rtet wuman, and yer faither sic an honest decent body, I might hae run ye in for smokin'. But if I catch ye at it again I wunna be sae lenient!'

Turning to Tam's mither in the door he said: 'By the by mistress, wha bides in that hoose in the howe, alang the Laich Road?'

'Oh,' says Tam's mither, wondering what the bobby was leading to. 'It's Mrs Lunan bides there.'

The bobby was now outside on the gravel, his brass buttons shining in the light from the open doorway, for it was now quite dark. 'Mrs Lunan,' says he, still quizzical, 'and do ye think she wad hae seen onybody suspicious, or could gie us ony information?'

Tam's mither began to tremble with excitement. 'Oh I hardly think so,' she said, trying to seem unconcerned, 'she's a bittie frae the road and disna see mony strangers.'

'Ah weel,' replied the bobby, 'but I'd better look in and see her onywye. Gweed nicht mistress!'

The policeman was scarcely astride his bicycle when Mrs Lunan burst in on Tam's folk from the darkness. They had been watching the rear-light on the bobby's bike as he sped down the brae. All had seemed lost but now they crowded round Mrs Lunan in the lighted doorway, to see what could be done.

'Run wifie,' cried Tam's mither, exasperated, 'fly hame as fast as ye can, the bobby has been here and he's just left, and he's on the road tae your hoose noo. Run wifie, for heaven's sake run!'

'Michty mee!' cried the woman, 'I meant tae borrow something, but that doesna matter noo. Michty mee! Oor hen's still on the table, or what's left o't!' And away she flew, clambering over the dyke like a schoolgirl, lost in the darkness.

It was touch and go: the bobby on his bike round by the road, the woman on her feet across the wet fields. The bobby had a few minutes' start ahead of her and she had another dyke to jump, and a deep ditch lay in her path.

Wee Tam could see the bobby's light as he moved along the Laich Road, but he could only guess how the woman fared in the darkness. The bobby had a gate to open at the end of the cart-track that led to the cottage. Tam closed the lobby door to shut in the light and waited. It wouldn't do to let the bobby know they were watching. It was touch and go . . .

It was close on midnight when Mrs Lunan went panting back to Tam's mither with the news. 'Michty mee,' she gasped, 'I got hame first but just in time. It was a near thing I can tell ye. I was like tae faint and fair oot o' breath or I reached the door. I put the hen oot o' sight in the dresser, double quick. I just had time tae get my breath back when the bobby rapped on the door. I closed the lobby door so's he couldna see my face in the licht, and he never cam' ben the hoose, so he never noticed my weet shoes and stockin's. Thank heavens he didna find us oot. We wunna hae tae try that again wifie!'

Tam's mither was relieved. 'Na faith ye,' she said, 'but hoo's yer man, Mrs Lunan?'

'He's fine,' said the woman, 'but he doesna ken a thing aboot it. He's sound asleep and he thinks I bocht the hen, me that hardly has a copper penny tae clap on anither.'

'And yer bairns, Mrs Lunan; are they asleep as weel?'

'Aye. I bedded them a' doon afore I cam' up here the first time and I hinna heard a myowt fae them since than.'

Tam's mither gave her a brimming glass of Dr Watson's Tonic Stout: 'Just to cheer you up wifie,' as she said, while the froth flew from the uncorked bottle.

Wee Tam went back to the lamp glass and relit his cigarette. His old man had gone to bed but he stopped snoring immediately and raised himself on his elbow, blinking at the light. 'Ony tae in the pot wuman?' says he, looking at his wife. 'No I dinna want the stout, nae at this time o' nicht, juist a drap tae. So that was whaur the hen cam' frae, auld Grimshaw. Weel weel, she was a tasty bird onywye!'

And then he turned on Wee Tam, now seated on a kitchen chair with *Robinson Crusoe*, the fag reek rising above the open pages. 'But ye'll hae tae watch yer smokin' ma loon, and if ye dinna come tae the byre when I want ye I'll tell the bobby ye've been at it again, ye wee rascal!'

The old blackmailer, Tam thought, but it should have taught the women a lesson.

The Wild Geese

EMIL PACHOLEK

The lands of Kincaple flowed gently down from the high grounds of Strathkinness, down and down in a run of green and gradual undulations.

The farm itself, a clutter of old, sandstone buildings, had been built into the slope of the last of the waves of hills, then below it, the ground spread itself flat and wide and fertile, right down to the marshlands that skirted the River Eden.

It was in one of the bottom fields, that one that was nearest to the fringes of whispering reeds and rushes, that Robbie and McPhee built the hide.

They'd worked well that Sunday, trailing long branches down from the Den Wood across the stubble field. It was hard and heavy going, and the field was wet with late October dampness.

Their leather boots were soaked and heavy, but they'd long since stopped caring about that.

The plan! That was all that mattered! That was all they thought about . . .

They rammed the bigger branches on end into the clay ground, in a rough circle just big enough to hold the pair of them. Then, in between the main branches, they threaded smaller ones, and reeds and clumps of grass, leaving but a small

120

entrance gap to wriggle into, and a couple of little slits to peep out of!

All morning it took them, and well into the afternoon. But it was worth it. The hide was near perfect.

'Can you see in?' called Robbie in a coarse whisper to McPhee, who stood outside.

'Not a sign of you!' came the tinker boy's hushed reply.

It was a strange them whispering, for the whole field was empty but for the pair of them, and the nearest houses were across the estuary in Guardbridge, over a mile away!

But dark deeds were afoot, and secrecy was all important.

'What about the grain?' whispered McPhee.

'There's a bin in the stables with loads of the stuff,' said Robbie. 'I'll get a bagful on my way back.'

'And the . . . the . . .' McPhee paused to look around before he dared say the word. His dark eyes shone with the devilment. 'And the whisky?'

Robbie grinned.

'My mother has some in the press. I'll get it tonight.'

'So it's tonight then?' asked McPhee.

Robbie looked up at the pale, silver sky. There was no cloud and already a big moon hung up in the east, shining like a half-crown.

'There'll be loads of light tonight. We'll see them fine!'

And so it was arranged.

The plan they'd worked out at the potato picking through the week was ready to be put to the test.

They'd been taking their break together, lying on their backs in the drills in the field up by the Den Wood when they'd come swinging over – the geese!

'It'd be a fine thing getting a couple of them,' Robbie had said, aiming and firing both barrels of an imaginary twelve-bore at the leading bird.

They'd watched the skein circle, lower and lower, cautious, looking out for any sign of danger. Round they went, and again in a wide sweep, but lower and lower all the time. Then, together, the flock had settled down into the barley stubble of the bottom field.

'We'd need some sort of a hide,' McPhee had said. 'Then we could sit in it at night and wait until they were close –'

'And grab them!' Robbie had cried. 'But . . . but they'd rise before we were near . . .'

There was a long silence as they both let the thoughts race through their minds.

'But what if we doped them, somehow,' Robbie had said. 'Then they'd be that bit slower in taking off . . .'

'Aye,' McPhee had said. 'But what could we dope them with . . .?'

The last pieces of the plan had fallen neatly into place.

And now they were ready to test it.

'I'll give you a hoot about midnight,' Robbie said as the two boys reached the top corner of the field at the foot of the Den Wood. And with no more than that, they parted. McPhee heading for the tinker's camp in the hollow half-way up the Den, and Robbie back to the stone cottage in the village of Kincaple.

But first through the farm. He had some grain to get.

Robbie slipped quiet as a cat through the farmyard, keeping his body close to the walls, edging up to corners, peeping round then scampering across the open spaces until he was at the stables.

He put his weight against the sliding door, hoping, hoping that the cast-iron wheels wouldn't squeak on the runners and give him away. But no sound came, and when the gap was a few inches wide, he squeezed inside, hauling it quietly closed behind him.

All the horses were in their stalls. Summer days had withered into autumn and were fallen and were gone, when the Clydesdales had spent their free hours turned loose in the lush, green park at the back of the farm. Days of capering and cantering, and nuzzling friendly like at each other's shoulders where the collars had pressed hard onto them when they'd been toiling through the long hours.

But the grass had lost its sweetness, and the horses had been moved inside, to the warmth of the deep straw, and the rich clover flavour of the hay in the mangers.

Two of the horses tossed their heads to see who the intruder was, but just for a moment, then it was back to tugging at a clump of hay and squeezing the sweet juices from it.

Robbie moved quietly down to the huge bins at the far end of the stable. He tugged at the lid, heaved it open, then dipped his hand inside. It was crushed oats. . . just what he was after!

There was a sack lying near and he picked it up, shaking the stoor from it in a great cloud. The dust tickled at his nose but he fought off the sneeze. No one must find him!

Then he delved a scoop into the bin and poured a cascade of oats into the open mouth of the sack. Then again. And again.

As he dipped in the fourth time, the voice came from behind him!

'And just what do you think you're up to, laddie?'

Robbie whirled and the scoop flew out of his hand, clattering to the floor and birling on the stone as he gaped, eyes wide, heart hammering.

From out of the end stall, from out of the shadows, came Dauve. Old Dauve, the strange quiet horseman who spent nearly every hour he had in the company of his pair of Clydesdales.

'Well, laddie – have you lost your tongue?'

Robbie's head reeled. The plan – he mustn't reveal the plan!

'It's for – it's for the hens!' he stammered out. 'We've got nothing to feed them on. Can I – can I take a wee bagful?

Dauve was close now, and his grey eyes stared hard at Robbie. They narrowed. For a long minute, Dauve said nothing. Then he made a sort of snorting noise and nodded.

'Aye, I suppose you can.'

Relief washed through Robbie, and he made to dash off with his plunder, but Dauve plucked the sack from his hand.

'But you'll have to earn this! You'll have to give me a hand with the horses.'

Kincaple Farm had four pairs of Clydesdale horses, and none looked better than Punch and Jeck, the two that old Dauve worked.

Their coats had more of a sheen, their harness more of a shine, and they even appeared to move better, with a self

123

assured swing to their walk that seemed to speak of the respect they had for the man.

It was a handsome sight seeing Dauve at the close of the day, sitting sideways up on Jeck with Punch in right behind, fair full of themselves, a real team and matched just right for each other.

He was a strange sort, dour and sullen, keeping himself to himself. He lived alone in a cramped little bothy in the village, but folks said it was more in the way of being a holiday home for Dauve, and that his real home was down in the stables for it was there that he spent most of his time, grooming his horses, talking to them, and polishing at the brass and leather of the harnesses.

Dauve handed Robbie a rope-handled, wooden bucket.

'You can fill that up with fine sawdust for me,' he said. 'And make sure it's dry stuff, mind!'

Robbie scurried round to the saw bench. The men had been making fence-stabs, and beneath the jagged, circular blade was a great mound of white sawdust. The boy delved the bucket into it and filled it to the brim.

When he returned to the stable, Dauve was at his horses. He was bathing their feet, washing the great plumed hooves. When he'd finished, he took handfuls of the sawdust and rubbed it into the long hair, working it right in. Then he brushed it all out and combed each foot in turn.

'What do you do that for? asked Robbie.

'It dries them,' answered Dauve, picking up each hoof in turn to inspect the hair and the shoe. 'The sawdust dries the hair. Makes a grand like job.'

Dauve picked at a hoof, coaxing out a stone.

'It's all a question of care,' he said. 'You mind that when you're older and you're working a pair of horse for yourself.'

Robbie grinned.

'But it'll not be horse then, Dauve. The farm'll be all tractors by that time.'

Dauve straightened up and for a moment, a strange look seemed to come on him – a far away look, either remembering days gone by or imagining days yet to come, Robbie wasn't sure.

Then Dauve snatched up Robbie's bag of oats and tossed it to him.

'Get away with you,' was all he said.

When he reached his cottage, Robbie didn't go in straight away. Instead, he went into the wash-house next door. He took a pail and poured the crushed oats into it, then hid it behind the fat, black boiler.

Then he gave his boots a quick brush with the broom, stuck his hands deep into his pockets and whistled as he sauntered, all innocent like, round the corner and home.

'And just where on earth have you been?' His mother's words rattled like hail as she met him at the door. 'Nothing inside your belly since breakfast! You'll have been with that McPhee, I'll bet – and up to some mischief or other!'

Robbie made his eyes go wide, and looked up at his mother.

'I've been helping Dauve, Mum,' he said. 'He wanted a hand with his horses.'

Robbie's mother looked hard at him for a moment.

'I'd have thought Dauve was able to look after his horses just fine without your assistance!'

But then, with a light skelp at his head, she smiled.

'Come on,' she said. 'There's some stewed hare in the oven – you're bound to be starving.'

Seconds later, the dish was out of the oven at the side of the fire, and before him, hot and steaming up into his face.

Robbie drew the sweet smell deep inside him, savouring the mouth-watering scent of it all.

'There's nothing to beat stewed hare, Mum,' he said, dipping a chunk of bread into the rich gravy. 'Except maybe,' he added, 'a nice roast goose.'

Robbie smiled a secret little smile to himself.

After he'd shut away the hens for the night, and filled up with sticks and coal, and done all the rest of his chores, Robbie put the final stages of his plan into action.

His mother was sitting by the fire in the living-room, darning a new heel into a sock. She looked up over the top of her

spectacles as the boy came through from the kitchen and her eyes opened wide with surprise.

'I've made you some tea!' Robbie announced, pouring what he'd spilt in the saucer back into the cup.

His mother beamed into a smile and shook her head in amazement.

'My, Robbie,' she exclaimed, putting her darning to one side, 'How lovely!'

"It's my pleasure, Mum,' declared Robbie grandly.

He sat by the fender, watching his mother sip at the brew. There was sugar in it — she took none — and the water hadn't been brought fully to the boil, giving it a coarse, raw sort of taste that fair scraped at the palate. But his mother said nothing, just sipped at it with a look of pleasure and contentment on her.

'Would you like some more?' Robbie asked when the last of it was gone. His mother shook her head — but not too much.

'No thank you, Robbie — that was just lovely.'

'Well, you bide where you are, Mum, and I'll wash the cup for you.'

And with that, the boy left, closing the door behind him and just missing the smile that tugged at the corners of his mother's mouth.

In the kitchen, Robbie rushed into action.

He eased open the press door and there it was — the whisky bottle! He carried it carefully in two hands over to the table, eased off the cork, and poured its entire contents into a jug.

Then he took the teapot and at the sink, half filled up the empty bottle with tea. Then he topped it up with water until the colour was just right, and rammed the cork back in.

His hands trembled as he slid the whisky bottle back to its place on the shelf in the press.

After that, he took the torch, let himself silently out of the kitchen door, and hurried as much as he dared with the full jug of whisky.

In the wash-house, he poured the whisky into the bucket of crushed oats and was back in the kitchen in seconds, whistling loudly and rattling at the cup and saucer in the sink.

Unaware of it all, his mother still sat darning in the living-room. sucking at a peppermint, trying to rid her palate of the taste of the tea.

As he lay in bed that night, Robbie's heart seemed to pound away inside him like the mill at threshing time!

The plan! The plan! The plan! His head fairly thundered with the thought of it.

He'd left the curtains open, and outside, the moon rose full and gleaming above the trees, painting all the branches with silver.

It was a fine night. A perfect night. And when he heard the geggle-gaggle calls from a skein of geese, flying over towards the estuary, it seemed to him like it was an omen, and Robbie's heart beat all the faster.

He heard the clock in the lobby strike half past nine, then ten . . .

Nearly an hour later, he heard his mother give the fire its final poke for the night, and a short time later, the door of her room gave a click.

The silence!

The clock struck eleven-thirty – and Robbie swung out of bed. He put his clothes on over the top of his pyjamas, carried his boots in his hand, eased up the window and was out!

He paused for a moment or two as he tied his laces, listening at the window, but there was no sound from within. Robbie crept into the wash-house, felt for the bucket in the black, found it and was off!

He'd done it!

The sky was scattered with stars and the light from the moon bathed the whole countryside in silver as Robbie ran along the track that led to the Den.

His shadow jiggled like a puppet before him, dancing merrily over the ground.

It seemed as if the whole world was asleep, and when he stopped to rest and change the bucket to his other hand, Robbie heard no sound other than the rush of his own breathing.

The Den Wood lay before him in the hollow like a sleeping dog, growing steadily larger as he loped towards it.

And then he was there!

Robbie cupped his hands to his lips and blew into the gap between his thumbs. His owl-hoot signal carried far into the silent wood, then again.

A few seconds later, an answering hoot came clear, and then McPhee himself was stepping out of the shadows. Under an arm, he carried two sticks.

'All right?' asked McPhee quietly.

'Aye,' Robbie whispered back. 'And yourself?'

'They never heard a thing,' grinned McPhee. 'Come on, let's get going! I've brought a couple of sticks – here's hoping we need them!'

The two boys hurried, crouched low, down the length of the field, keeping close to the line of the hawthorn hedging that ran almost all the way to the riverside.

It seemed as if they could see for miles in the strange light, and soon they could see the outline of the hide down by the reeds.

As they neared it, Robbie suddenly stopped, holding McPhee by the arm.

'Look!' he breathed. 'In the field! Dozens of them!'

McPhee followed the line of Robbie's jabbing finger and there, in the stubble, between the hide and the edge of the rushes, were the plump shapes of a whole flock of greylag geese! Robbie bit at his lip in excitement!

Almost crawling now, the two boys reached the cover of a line of reeds. They eased their way along, moving the pail a foot or so in front, then wriggled forward. Easing and wriggling . . . easing and wriggling . . .

They were only a few yards away from the safety of their hide now.

Silently, hardly daring to breathe, they stole forward, keeping the hide between themselves and the geese.

And suddenly, they were there!

The two boys squeezed in together, nudging and poking each other in silent delight at their triumph.

McPhee bent back some of the grass from the hide. Robbie

dipped into the pail and took out a handful of the mixture. The whisky had soaked right into the crushed oats and its pungent smell filled the hide.

Carefully, so carefully, he tossed a little out onto the stubble before them. Then again. And then some more. If the geese saw the movement, they'd be off and the whole plan ruined! Each handful was a risk they hardly dared take, but luck held, and soon Robbie had emptied the bucket and all the mixture lay in the stubble just a few feet in front of the hide!

The two boys crouched at their peepholes and the long wait began . . .

Outside, the geese cackled softly to each other, some resting with their heads tucked in below their wings, some on guard around the edges of the flocks, and some feeding in the stubble.

But as yet, none fed on the mixture!

It was cold now, and Robbie's legs began to ache.

Although the sky was clear, there was no frost, but the dampness on the ground seemed to seep right into him.

McPhee nudged him in the arm.

'Here!' he whispered in the darkness of the hide, and he fed one of the sticks into Robbie's grip.

Robbie returned to the peephole.

Some of the geese seemed closer, moving around, foraging in the stubble for food.

One came very near, waddling past less than four feet from them and Robbie saw a quick glint of the moon in its eye, and could make out the lighter colour of its feet and its bill. It didn't eat the oats, didn't even see the stuff, it seemed.

But it was followed by another bird, and this one did see the grain. The goose dipped its head down into the stubble before them and the boys could hear its bill clacking as it tasted the food.

Then again, and this time, it made pleased little noises in its throat as it stretched its neck upwards and ate. Its pleasure was sensed by another goose, and soon, four of them were round the mixture, scooping it up into their bills.

Robbie gripped his fingers into McPhee's arm. McPhee was tense, scarcely breathing.

And still the geese guzzled into the oats, shovelling their bills into it, and it seemed to the two boys that there was a sort of unruliness creeping in.

The birds seemed to be well taken with the stuff.

Was it working? Was it the whisky that was making them greedy, almost reckless to get more? What if they rushed them now?

The question raced as fast as their pulses.

But no — best to wait . . . give them time . . . let them eat more . . . let them eat the lot!

The two boys watched, dry-mouthed, at their peepholes.

The four geese were almost squabbling with each other, ruffling out their wings, barging at each other, craning their long necks forward, snapping for the food.

It was near time . . .

McPhee tugged at Robbie's sleeve, and silently, stealthily, they crept out of the gap at the rear of the hide.

Robbie felt the stick heavy in his hand as they inched round. Slowly . . . slowly . . . slowly . . .

And then, together, they pounced!

Robbie and McPhee launched themselves forward!

In an instant, the night was filled with alarm calls as scores of wings thrashed the air, pushing, pushing, pushing away from the sudden danger!

Robbie dived to the ground!

Whether it was the whisky, or whether it was the sudden fright that froze it, Robbie never knew — but just as he hit the stubble, his hand fell across a goose's neck! His fingers clasped it instantly!

Robbie felt it come alive in his grip and struggle, and the wings clattered and crashed in panic, cracking him about the head.

But he didn't let go!

His fingers were clamped around the thick neck and were there to stay! Then he swung the stick and felt it thud onto the goose's back, stunning it. And again . . . and again . . .

With both hands now, Robbie gave a quick jerk, pulling at the bird's neck. He felt it give.

The goose fluttered and flapped on its back, but its life was already gone.

As he rose to his feet in triumph, Robbie saw McPhee thrash out at another bird, and it too was taken.

All around them, geese cackled into the night, flickering like witches across the face of the moon.

But two would never rise again.

Robbie and McPhee sent yells of delight into the air around them.

All the way home, Robbie thrilled to the weight of the dead goose in his hand. It was huge and fat and heavy, and with every step, the boy could feel the excitement rush up in him. He'd got a goose, a real live goose – at least, it had been!

He chuckled to himself as he imagined his mother's face in the morning. The best thing would be to put it on the kitchen table for her to find first thing!

Then he could help to pluck it, and singe off the fine feathers that they missed, and prepare it and cook it and carve it . . . his mouth fair watered at the thought!

Robbie coaxed up his window and swung quietly inside dragging the weight of the goose after him. He took off his boots and tip-toed through the kitchen, trailing the great dead bird behind him.

He pushed open the door, and as it swung wide, he saw that the room was bright with light.

Robbie blinked, and saw before him his mother, her arms folded, her face clouded, her foot tapping in time to her temper!

Behind her, was the large, forbidding figure of Sergeant Baxter – the Local Police Force himself!

For what seemed an age, no one moved and no one spoke.

The boy with the dead goose stared up at the woman and the policeman – and the woman and the policeman stared down at the boy with the dead goose!

And then the silence was shattered by Robbie's mother!

'Just what have you been up to?' she shrieked. 'You've had me worried sick! I woke up, went through to your room to make sure you were tucked in and – and nothing!'

Her voice rose and rose until it could rise no more! She paused for breath and started all over again!

'Worried sick, I was! I – I've even been up to the phone-box and poor Sergeant Baxter's come pedalling all the way up here on his bike!'

Robbie swallowed hard, then held out the goose. Its head lay dropped over his arm, and spots of blood dripped like sealing wax from its bill onto the floor.

'Goose?' howled his mother. 'I'll give you goose, my lad!'

She lunged forward to grab the boy, but Robbie sidestepped and his mother was left clutching the dead bird by the throat! With a yowl, she dropped it to the floor!

Robbie made to jink past her, but she whipped round and caught him by the ear.

Sergeant Baxter cleared his throat and tucked his notebook back into the top pocket of his tunic.

'Ah well, now,' he said to Robbie's mother. 'I see you have the matter well in hand. I'll just be getting down the road again . . .'

He buttoned the top button of his uniform, and cleared his throat again. Then he wiped at his mouth with his hand.

'Aye,' he said, smacking his lips. 'It's a right cold night, is it not . . .?'

Robbie's mother relaxed her grip on the boy's ear and turned to the policeman.

'Oh, Sergeant Baxter,' she said. 'How thoughtless of me. Would you – would you care for a wee dram to warm you up on the journey?'

The sergeant pretended to be surprised at the offer.

'Oh, how kind you are,' he smiled, licking at his lips again. 'Well now, a wee dram sounds like a grand idea . . .'

Robbie, already in fear of the hiding that was sure to come, looked on like a doomed rabbit.

His mother reached into the press for the whisky bottle, uncorked it, and poured a large measure into a glass.

'Your very good health!' declared Sergeant Baxter grandly. And he tipped the lot down his throat.

Robbie closed his eyes.

Alicky's Watch

FRED URQUHART

Alexander's watch stopped on the morning of his mother's funeral. The watch had belonged to his grandfather and had been given to Alexander on his seventh birthday two years before. It had a large tarnished metal case and he could scarcely see the face through the smoky celluloid front, but Alexander treasured it. He carried it everywhere, and whenever anybody mentioned the time Alexander would take out the watch, look at it, shake his head with the senile seriousness of some old man he had seen, and say: 'Ay, man, but is that the time already?'

And now the watch had stopped. The lesser tragedy assumed proportions which had not been implicit in the greater one. His mother's death seemed far away now because it had been followed by such a period of hustle and bustle: for the past three days the tiny house had been crowded with people coming and going. There had been visits from the undertakers, visits to the drapers for mourning-bands and black neckties. There had been an unwonted silence with muttered 'sshs' whenever he or James spoke too loudly. And there had been continual genteel bickerings between his two grandmothers, each of them determined to uphold the dignity of death in the house, but each of them equally determined to have her own way in the arrangements for the funeral.

133

The funeral was a mere incident after all that had gone before. The stopping of the watch was the real tragedy. At two o'clock when the cars arrived, Alexander still had not got over it. He kept his hand in his pocket, fingering it all through the short service conducted in the parlour while slitherings and muffled knocks signified that the coffin was being carried out to the hearse. And he was still clutching it with a small, sweaty hand when he took his seat in the first car between his father and his Uncle Jimmy.

His mother was to be buried at her birthplace, a small mining village sixteen miles out from Edinburgh. His father and his maternal grandmother, Granny Peebles, had had a lot of argument about this. His father had wanted his mother to be cremated, but Granny Peebles had said: 'But we have the ground, Sandy! We have the ground all ready waiting at Beth-niebrig. It would be a pity not to use it. There's plenty of room on top of her father for poor Alice. And there'll still be enough room left for me – God help me! – when I'm ready to follow them.'

'But the expense, Mrs Peebles, the expense,' his father had said. 'It'll cost a lot to take a funeral all that distance, for mind you we'll have to have a lot o' carriages, there's such a crowd o' us.'

'It winna be ony mair expensive than payin' for cremation,' Granny Peebles had retorted. 'I dinna hold wi' this cremation, onywye, it's ungodly. And besides the ground's there waiting.'

The arguments had gone back and forth, but in the end Mrs Peebles had won. Though it was still rankling in his father's mind when he took his seat in the front mourning-car. 'It's a long way, Jimmy,' he said to his brother. 'It's a long way to take the poor lass. She'd ha'e been better, I'm thinkin', to have gone up to Warriston Crematorium.'

'Ay, but Mrs Peebles had her mind made up aboot that,' Uncle Jimmy said. 'She's a tartar, Mrs Peebles, when it comes to layin' doon the law.'

Although Alexander was so preoccupied with his stopped watch he wondered, as he had so often wondered in the past, why his father and his Uncle Jimmy called her Mrs Peebles when they called Granny Matheson 'Mother'. But he did not dare ask.

'"We have the ground at Bethniebrig, Sandy,"' mimicked Uncle Jimmy. '"And if we have the ground we must use it. There'll still be room left for me when my time comes." The auld limmer, I notice there was no word aboot there bein' room for you when *your* time comes, m'man!'

Alexander's father did not answer. He sat musing in his new-found dignity of widowerhood; his back was already bowed with the responsibility of being father and mother to two small boys. He was only thirty-one.

All the way to Bethniebrig Cemetery Alexander kept his hand in his pocket, clasping the watch. During the burial service, where he was conscious of being watched and afterwards when both he and James were wept over and kissed by many strange women, he did not dare touch his treasure. But on the return journey he took the watch from his pocket and sat with it on his knee. His father was safely in the first car with Mr Ogilvie, the minister, and his mother's uncles, Andrew and Pat. Alexander knew that neither his Uncle Jimmy nor his Uncle Jimmy's chum, Ernie, would mind if he sat with the watch in his hand.

'Is it terrible bad broken, Alicky?' asked James, who was sitting between Ernie and his mother's cousin, Arthur.

'Ay,' Alexander said.

'Never mind, laddie, ye can aye get a new watch, but ye cannie get a new —'

Ernie's observation ended with a yelp of pain. Uncle Jimmy grinned and said: 'Sorry, I didnie notice your leg was in my way!'

The cars were going quicker now than they had gone on the way to the cemetery. Alicky did not look out of the windows; he tinkered with his watch, winding and rewinding it, holding it up to his ear to see if there was any effect.

'Will it never go again, Alicky?' James said.

'Here, you leave Alicky alone and watch the rabbits,' Ernie said, pulling James on his knee. 'My God, look at them! All thae white tails bobbin' aboot! Wish I had a rifle here, I'd soon take a pot-shot at them.'

135

'Wish we had a pack o' cards,' said Auntie Liz's young man, Matthew. 'We could have a fine wee game o' Solo.'

'I've got my pack in my pocket,' Ernie said, raking for them. 'What aboot it, lads?'

'Well —' Uncle Jimmy looked at Cousin Arthur; then he shook his head. 'No, I dinnie think this is either the time or the place.'

'Whatever you say, pal!' Ernie gave all his attention to James, shooting imaginary rabbits, crooking his finger and making popping sounds with his tongue against the roof of his mouth.

The tram-lines appeared, then the huge villas at Newington. The funeral cars had to slow down when Clerk Street and the busier thoroughfare started. James pressed his nose against the window to gaze at the New Victoria which had enormous posters billing a 'mammoth Western spectacle'.

'Jings, but I'd like to go to that,' he said. 'Wouldn't you, Alicky?'

But Alicky did not look out at the rearing horses and the Red Indians in full chase. He put his watch to his ear and shook it violently for the fiftieth time.

'I doubt it's no good, lad,' Uncle Jimmy said. 'It's a gey auld watch, ye ken. It's seen its day and generation.'

The blinds were up when they got back, and the table was laid for high tea. Granny Matheson and Granny Peebles were buzzing around, carrying plates of cakes and tea-pots. Auntie Liz took the men's coats and hats and piled them on the bed in the back bedroom. Alicky noticed that the front room where the coffin had been was still shut. There was a constrained air about everybody as they stood about in the parlour. They rubbed their hands and spoke about the weather. It was only when Granny Matheson cried: 'Sit in now and get your tea,' that they began to return to normal.

'Will you sit here, Mr Ogilvie, beside me?' she said. 'Uncle Andrew, you'll sit there beside Liz, and Uncle Pat over there.'

'Sandy, you'll sit here beside me,' Granny Peebles called from the other end of the table. 'And Uncle George'll sit next to Cousin Peggy, and Arthur, you can sit —'

'Arthur's to sit beside Ernie,' Granny Matheson cut in. 'Now,

I think that's us all settled, so will you pour the tea at your end, m'dear?'

'I think we'd better wait for Mr Ogilvie,' Granny Peebles said stiffly. And she inclined her head towards the minister, smoothing the black silk of her bosom genteelly.

Alicky and James had been relegated to a small table, which they were glad was nearer to their Granny Matheson's end of the large table. They bowed their heads with everyone else when Mr Ogilvie started to pray, but after the first few solemn seconds Alicky allowed himself to peek from under his eyelashes at the dainties on the sideboard. He was sidling his hand into his pocket to feel his watch when Tiddler, the cat, sprang on to the sideboard and nosed a large plate of boiled ham. Alicky squirmed in horror, wondering whether it would be politic to draw attention to the cat and risk being called 'a wicked ungodly wee boy for not payin' attention to what the minister's sayin' about yer puir mammy,' or whether it would be better to ignore it. But Mr Ogilvie saved the situation. He stopped in the middle of a sentence and said calmly in his non-praying voice: 'Mrs Peebles, I see that the cat's up at the boiled ham. Hadn't we better do something about it?'

After tea the minister left, whisky and some bottles of beer were produced for the men, and port wine for the ladies. The company thawed even more. Large, jovial Uncle Pat, whose red face was streaming with sweat, unbuttoned his waistcoat, saying: 'I canna help it, Georgina, if I dinna loosen my westkit I'll burst the buttons. Ye shouldna gi'e fowk sae much to eat!'

'I'm glad you tucked in and enjoyed yourself,' Granny Peebles said, nodding her head regally.

'Mr Ogilvie's a nice man,' Granny Matheson said, taking a cigarette from Uncle Jimmy. 'But he kind o' cramps yer style, doesn't he? I mean it's no' like havin' one o' yer own in the room. Ye've aye got to be on yer p's and q's wi' him, mindin' he's a minister.'

'Ye havenie tellt us who was all at the cemetery,' she said, blowing a vast cloud of smoke in the air and wafting it off with a plump arm. 'Was there a lot o' Bethniebrig folk there?'

'Ay, there was a good puckle,' Uncle Pat said. 'I saw auld Alex Whitten and young Tam Forbes and —'

'Oh, ay, they fair turned out in force,' Uncle Jimmy said.

'And why shouldn't they?' Granny Peebles said. 'After all, our family's had connections with Bethniebrig for generations. I'm glad they didnie forget to pay their respects to puir Alice.' And she dabbed her eyes with a small handkerchief, which had never been shaken out of the fold.

'I must say it's a damned cauld draughty cemetery yon,' Uncle Andrew said. 'I was right glad when Mr Ogilvie stopped haverin' and we got down to business. I was thinkin' I'd likely catch my death o' cauld if he yapped on much longer.'

'Uncle Pat near got his death o' cauld, too,' Uncle Jimmy grinned. 'Didn't ye, auld yin?'

'Ay, ay, lad, I near did that!' Uncle Pat guffawed. 'I laid my tile hat ahint a gravestone at the beginnin' of the service and when it was ower I didna know where it was. Faith, we had a job findin' it.'

'Ay, we had a right search!' Uncle Jimmy said.

'It's a pity headstones havenie knobs on them for hats,' Auntie Liz said.

'Really, Lizzie Matheson!' cried Granny Peebles.

Auntie Liz and the younger women began to clear the table, but Alexander noticed that Auntie Liz did not go so often to the scullery as the others. She stood with dirty plates in her hands, listening to the men who had gathered around the fire. Uncle Pat had his feet up on the fender, his large thighs spread wide apart. 'It's a while since we were all gathered together like this,' he remarked, finishing his whisky and placing the glass with an ostentatious clatter on the mantelpiece. 'I think the last time was puir Willie's funeral two years syne.'

'Ay, it's a funny thing but it's aye funerals we seem to meet at,' Uncle Andrew said.

'Well, well, there's nothin' sae bad that hasna got some guid in it,' Uncle Pat said. 'Yes, Sandy lad, I'll take another wee nippie, thank ye!' And he watched his nephew with a benign expression as another dram was poured for him. 'Well, here's your guid health again, Georgina! I'm needin' this, I can tell ye, for it was a cauld journey doon this mornin' frae Aberdeen, and it was a damned sight caulder standin' in that cemetery.'

Alexander squeezed his way behind the sofa into the corner beside the whatnot. Looking to see that he was unnoticed, he drew the watch cautiously from his pocket and tinkered with it. As the room filled with tobacco smoke the talk and laughter got louder.

'Who was yon wi' the long brown moth-eaten coat?' Uncle Jimmy said. 'He came up and shook hands wi' me after the service. I didnie ken him from Adam, but I said howdyedo. God, if he doesnie drink he should take doon his sign!'

'Och, thon cauld wind would make anybody's nose red,' Matthew said.

'Ay, and who was yon hard case in the green bowler?' Ernie said.

'Ach, there was dozens there in bowlers,' Uncle Jimmy said.

'Ay, but this was a *green* bowler!'

Uncle Jimmy guffawed. 'That reminds me o' the one about the old lady and the minister. Have ye heard it?'

Alexander prised open the case of the watch, then he took a pin from a small box on the whatnot and inserted it delicately into the works. There was loud laughter, and Ernie shouted above the others: 'Ay, but have ye heard the one about –?'

'What are ye doin', Alicky?' James whispered, leaning over the back of the sofa.

'Shuttup,' Alexander said in a low voice, bending over the watch and poking gently at the tiny wheels.

'I dinnie see why women can't go to funerals, too,' Auntie Liz said. 'You men ha'e all the fun.'

'Lizzie Matheson!' Granny Peebles cried. 'What a like thing to say! I thought ye were going to help your mother wash the dishes?'

It was going! Alicky could hardly believe his eyes. The small wheels were turning – turning slowly, but they were turning. He held the watch to his ear, and a slow smile of pleasure came over his face.

'What are you doing there behind the sofa?'

Alexander and James jumped guiltily. 'I've got my watch to go!' Alicky cried to his father. 'Listen!'

'Alexander Matheson, have you nothing better to do than tinker wi' an auld watch?' Granny Peebles said. 'I'm surprised at ye,' she said as she swept out.

Abashed, Alicky huddled down behind the sofa. James climbed over and sat beside him. They listened to the men telling stories and laughing, but when the room darkened and the voices got even louder the two little boys yawned. They whispered together. 'Go on, you ask him,' James pleaded. 'You're the auldest!'

James went on whispering. Beer bottles were emptied, the laughter and the family reminiscences got wilder. And presently, plucking up courage, Alexander went to his father and said: 'Can James and I go to the pictures?'

There was a short silence.

'Alexander Matheson,' his father cried. 'Alexander Matheson, you should be ashamed o' yersel' sayin' that and your puir mother no' cauld in her grave.'

'Och, let the kids go, Sandy,' Uncle Jimmy said. 'It's no' much fun for them here.'

'We're no' here for fun,' Alexander's father said, but his voice trailed away indecisively.

'You go and put the case to your granny, lad, and see what she says,' Uncle Jimmy said. He watched the two boys go to the door, then looking round to see that Mrs Peebles was still out of the room, he said: 'Your Granny Matheson.'

Five minutes later, after a small lecture, Granny Matheson gave them the entrance money to the cinema. 'Now remember two things,' she said, showing them out. 'Don't run, and be sure to keep your bonnets on.'

'Okay,' Alicky said.

They walked sedately to the end of the street. Alicky could feel the watch ticking feebly in his pocket, and his fingers caressed the metal case. When they got to the corner they looked round, then they whipped off their bonnets, stuffed them in their pockets, and ran as quickly as they could to the cinema.

Glossary of Scots Words

aboot	about
ahint	behind
alang	along
ane	one
auld yin	old one
ay	yes
aye	always
ben room	inner room (of 2-roomed cottage)
birling	spinning
bittie	bit
blaw	blow
bocht	bought
brae	hillside
bree	soup
breeks	trousers
burn	small stream
brig	bridge
but-and-ben	a two-roomed cottage
buckie	snail
byre	cow-shed
cam' ben	came inside
cauld	cold
chauving	struggling
couching	lying in its lair
crater	creature
croft	smallholding; piece of farming land smaller than a farm
cutty	short tobacco-pipe
dinnie	do not
dominie	schoolmaster
dram	drink of whisky
faither	father
ferlies	strange sights

141

fine near	very close
Fit's wrang?	What's wrong?
fowk	folk, people
frae	from
gab	chat
gear	luggage
ghaist	ghost
gey	very
gillie	man or boy who assists hunting or shooting party
going his own gait	going his own way
guddling	catching fish with the hands
gweed-he'rtet	good-hearted
gweed nicht	good night
hame	home
hauld your whisht	be quiet
havering	babbling, chattering, foolishly
Here a wee	Wait a minute
hoose	house
howe	vale, hollow
jalouse	guess, suspect
jeuked the school	played truant
jouked	escaped, dodged
kail-yard	kitchen-garden
laird	local landowner
limmer	rascal, bad boy
loon	boy
Losh!	exclamation, e.g. gosh! gracious!
mair	more
maister	master
messages	groceries
Michty mee!	another exclamation, e.g. goodness me!
midden	rubbish heap
mither	mother
mony	many
nicht	night
old bogle	phantom, goblin, bogyman
ony	any
onywye	anyway
oot	out
orra patched breeks	disreputable patched trousers
ower mony	too many
oxter	armpit or inside of arm

Glossary of Scots Words

peedie	little
puckle	small amount
puir	poor
ramping	raging
rasps	raspberries
richt	right
Sassenach	Englishman
scrimshanking	shirking one's duty
sharn	dung
shauchly	clumsily
shivers	small pieces
sic	such
skelp	slap
sluagh	crowd
smiddy	smithy
snibbed	dropped
steading	farmstead
stoor	dust
strathspey	a Scottish dance
swithered	dithered
tae	tea
thon	that
tile hat	top hat
tilt cart	covered wagon
trull	slut, slovenly woman
Turk's head	a kind of knot
tyke	mongrel
two years syne	two years ago
weet	wet
whaur	where
whins	gorse bushes
withoot	without
yon	yonder, that

Acknowledgements

The editor and publishers gratefully acknowledge permission to reproduce copyright material in this book:

'The Dreamer' and 'Discovery', from *The Nine Lives of Fankle the Cat* by George Mackay Brown, reproduced by permission of the Bodley Head;
'Icarus' and 'Tartan' by George Mackay Brown, from *A Time to Keep and Other Short Stories*, reprinted by permission of Chatto & Windus;
'Sunday Class' by Elspeth Davie, from *The Spark and Other Stories*, reprinted by permission of John Calder (Publishers) Ltd;
'The Consolation Prize' by Lavinia Derwent; from *The Noel Streatfield Birthday Story Book* (J. M. Dent), © Lavinia Derwent, 1976, reproduced by permission of the author;
'Jehovah's Joke' by Mollie Hunter; from *The Noel Streatfield Birthday Story Book* (J. M. Dent), reproduced by permission of A. M. Heath and Company Ltd;
'The Mystery of the Beehive' by Bernard Mac Laverty, from *Storyline Scotland 4*, reproduced by permission of the Longman Group Ltd;
'The Wild Ride in the Tilt Cart' and 'Sandy Macneil and His Dog' by Sorche Nic Leodhas, from *Gaelic Ghosts* (Bodley Head), reprinted by permission of A. M. Heath and Company Ltd;
'Silver Linings' by Joan Lingard, reproduced by permission of David Higham Associates Limited;
'The Wild Geese' by Emil Pacholek, from *Robbie*, reproduced by permission of André Deutsch Ltd;
'Three Fingers are Plenty' by Neil Paterson, from *And Delilah – Nine Stories*, © Neil Paterson 1951, reproduced by permission of Curtis Brown, London;
'The Blot' by Iain Crichton Smith, from *Short Stories from Scotland*, reprinted by permission of the author;
'Do You Believe in Ghosts?' by Iain Crichton Smith, from *On the Island*, reprinted by permission of Victor Gollancz Ltd;
'Touch and Go!' by David Toulmin, from *Hard Shining Corn* (Impulse), by permission of John Reid;
'Grumphie' by F. G. Turnbull, from *Kallee and Other Stories*, reprinted by permission of Rupert Crew Ltd;
'Alicky's Watch' by Fred Urquhart, from *The Last Sister* (Methuen Children's Books Ltd), reprinted by permission of Mrs Herta Ryder.

Every effort has been made to trace copyright holders. The editor and publishers apologize if they have inadvertently failed to acknowledge any copyright holders and would like to hear from them.